MW01104845

SOUTH BENTINCK SUMMER

Alvin Gauthier

 FriesenPress

One Printers Way
Altona, MB, R0G 0B0
Canada

www.friesenpress.com

ISBN
978-1-03-912328-1 (Hardcover)
978-1-03-912327-4 (Paperback)
978-1-03-912329-8 (eBook)

1. JUVENILE FICTION, NATURE & THE NATURAL WORLD

Distributed to the trade by The Ingram Book Company

Thank you

Alex, Barbara, Bert, Bud, Elyce, Florence, Nancy

. . . and all the nieces and nephews who find
this page in this book.

- Raymond Steinberg

ALVIN N. GAUTHIER

Shown with fish he caught in the Port Townsend Salmon Derby, 1947

ABOUT THE AUTHOR

Alvin Nelson Gauthier was my "Uncle Al," and he has always been one of my heroes. He was part of the household in which I grew up, and I learned much from him. He never attended college but was a man of letters, a voracious reader, and a productive writer. Although he was blinded by disease in his early twenties, he managed to gain in-depth knowledge of geography, natural science, literature, current politics, and more. He knew much about mathematics.

Shortly after he became blind, Uncle Al learned to read braille. I recall that he received large books in the mail without ink on the pages, only raised bumps in various patterns that he could read. He received and returned these books regularly for years. He must have read both fiction and nonfiction because he could talk and write about a wide range of subjects. When I had a question regarding something I was reading, Uncle Al was the person I asked. Two authors we discussed were Jack London and Jules Verne.

Uncle Al was a great baseball fan and listened to radio broadcasts of games played by his favorite team, the Seattle Rainiers. He could tell you about specific games, the players, and the standings of all the Pacific Coast League teams. When Major League Baseball expanded to the West Coast, he followed it just as intently, the only difference being that he now listened to the Los Angeles Dodgers' games.

He refused to let his blindness dictate how he lived his life. As he began to lose his sight, he enlisted the aid of friends and together they helped build the farmhouse that became our home. After he lost his sight, he continued to be productive physically as well as mentally. He regularly went into the woods beyond the pasture and felled trees, limbed them, and cut the wood into stove lengths for the kitchen range and the fireplace. He loved salmon fishing and caught many fish. He found ways to stay involved in his many interests, yet he also always made time to share his life with those around him, especially his niece and nephews.

Uncle Al was a great storyteller. The adventures he had before his blindness provided material for the many short stories, a novel, and a memoir he wrote. *South Bentinck Summer* is the only book he wrote for young adults. It chronicles the adventures of two brothers who spend their summer at a logging camp in British Columbia that is managed by their dad. It's a compelling story and includes fascinating descriptions of wildlife, plants, and the terrain of Western Canada.

Uncle Al died in 1968, but I'll never forget him or the things I learned from him. I believe your experience will be much like mine when you read his story. The fun and the facts and the story are there for you. And if you read a little bit between the lines, Uncle Al is there too.

Raymond Steinberg

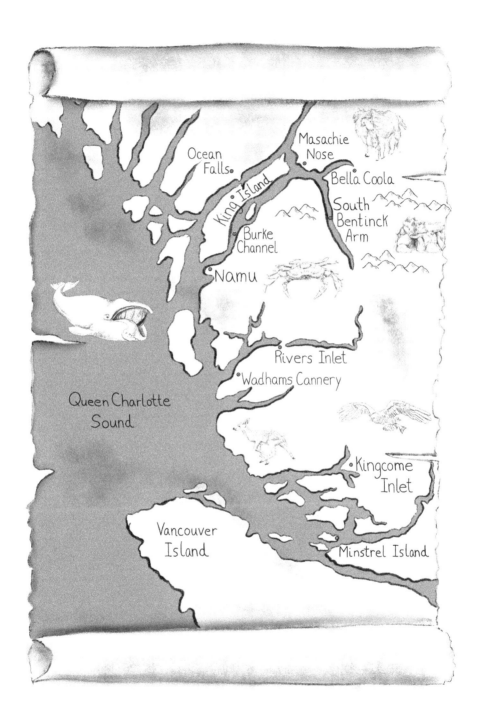

Table of Contents

Chapter 1

Vacation at the Logging Camp

Tommy stretched drowsily and yawned. Then he was wide awake. Surely it must be time to get up. It was after midnight before they got to bed, but he had been too excited to sleep very much. And there would be a million fascinating things to do here at Dad's logging camp halfway up the British Columbia coast on South Bentinck Arm. Sleeping seemed an awful waste of time—vacation wouldn't last forever.

Tommy's summer had gotten off to a wonderful start with the floatplane ride from Vancouver. There were high, jagged mountains to his right and the rolling hills of Vancouver Island to his left. Green islands and narrow waterways below them looked like the amazing scenery that Tommy had seen only on picture postcards. Several kids from Hastings Academy, his boarding school, were on the floatplane, all heading for their homes on the islands or along the inlets. They landed several times at places with exciting names: Whaletown, Minstrel Island, Kingcome Inlet, Wadhams Cannery, Namu, and finally, Ocean Falls with its big pulp and paper mill.

The boat ride to South Bentinck was exciting too. Eighty miles of narrow channels with great mountains bathing their feet in the *salt chuck*. It was dark when they passed Mesachie Nose and the mouth of Bella Coola Inlet. He remembered from history class that it was the place where Alexander Mackenzie had reached salt water on the first-ever overland crossing of the continent north of Mexico. The boat made a snake trail of pale phosphorescent flame when it chugged slowly through the glow of a hundred lights on fishing boats and buoys at the ends of long gill nets. Tommy wondered how the captain could tell which two lights belonged to any one net, but they got through without hitting any of them.

Tommy couldn't see much of the long narrow body of water off Burke Channel that was South Bentinck Arm. There were only vague shadows and the snow-tipped mountains sharply outlined against a black-velvet sky. He wanted to see his summer home--the mountains and South Bentinck--in daylight, but morning seemed a long time coming.

Tommy's older brother, Chet, was pressed hard against him in the narrow bunk filled with springy cedar boughs. Chet was 14 and kind of bossy. He would be grouchy if he was awakened too soon, so Tommy didn't move, even though it was hard to lie still when he was wide awake.

There was no window in the little room Dad had built for them at the corner of the storeroom off the logging-camp kitchen. A fellow couldn't even guess at the time, but through the thin board partition Tommy could hear someone moving in the cookhouse. Surely it must be near breakfast time.

Hastings Academy in Vancouver seemed a long way off, and the family farm on Lulu Island was even farther away. Tommy had been spending his summers at the farm with Uncle Phil and Aunt Martha for the last four years, ever since Mom died when he was six. The farm wasn't much of a place for a vacation. There were always chores, and there was no one to play with except for his little cousin Judy, and she wasn't much fun.

Tommy thought Chet had the best of it all. He had spent the last three summers with Dad up here on South Bentinck Arm. That would make this summer all the more pleasant for Tommy because Chet would know all the interesting things to see and to do, all the best places to fish and to swim.

A terrific clamor came from outside. It woke Chet. It would certainly wake every wild creature around the head of South Bentinck. Tommy was up and dressed while Chet was still trying to wipe the sleep out of his eyes and mumbling something about getting up in the middle of the night. Spike, a thin-faced flunky from the cookhouse, was pounding on a steel triangle with an iron bar when Tommy went outside. He knew days were long up here in June, but the sun hadn't yet climbed high enough to shine on the mountains across the water. Tommy realized the inlet was beautiful in the early morning, with calm water that was a more vivid green than the mountains it reflected. He saw loggers pouring out of the two big bunkhouses. They were mostly big men with overalls tucked into high caulked boots and rolled-up shirttails tucked through a strap at the back of the overalls.

Tommy was washing in ice-cold water when Dad and old Mr. Harris, the timekeeper, came out of the room they shared behind the office. They were the only ones who had taken time to shave. Spike was still pounding on the triangle to signal breakfast was ready when Chet came out and tested the water in a basin with one finger. Dad hurried over to him.

"Step on it, Chet," he snapped. "Remember, up here you will have to be on time for your meals. The cook is too busy to run a short-order house for you. Come along, Tommy."

Dad didn't sound cross exactly, but when he spoke in that tone no one gave him any back talk. He wasn't as big as most of the men in the camp, but he was strong and wiry, and he was smarter than any of them. *That's why he's the boss*, Tommy thought, as he followed him into the cookhouse.

Dad slipped into a chair at the head of a long table. Benches ran the whole length of it on either side. He motioned Tommy to a seat on the end of the one to his left. Loggers hurried in, their caulked boots making clicking sounds on the slivered floor planks. Spike rushed around, putting platters of food and pots of coffee on the table. He was a skinny kid not much older than Chet. Peg Leg, the cook, hopped nimbly around the big range flipping flapjacks. Tommy thought it wasn't polite to make fun of him because he had lost a leg, but that was the only name anyone seemed to know for him.

Breakfast was a hurry-up affair. The men ate huge quantities of bacon, eggs, and flapjacks. They didn't waste any time, and there wasn't much talking. Big Bill Brannigan, the hook tender, sat beside Tommy. He was a huge square block of a man with long black hair and twinkling eyes. He grinned down at Tommy.

"It's easy to see that you and Chet are Red Baldwin's kids," Bill said, eyeing Tommy from top to bottom. "The same carrot tops and hazel eyes. Red hasn't as many freckles as you, though, and I doubt that he was ever so chubby. Chet is more his build: long and lanky."

Chet was slipping onto the bench across from Tommy. He did look like Dad. In three or four years, he'd probably be as big as Dad. But Chet had been chubby too when he was ten. *I'll grow out of it*, Tommy told himself.

Some of the men were leaving, and Tommy had hardly gotten started on his flapjacks and honey. They were delicious. He mustn't forget to tell Peg Leg how much he liked them.

Soon Dad finished his coffee and got up. "If you go up where we are working, don't let Tommy get too close to the lines or the fallers, Chet," he said, and hurried away. Chet mumbled something about playing nursemaid but not until Dad was outside.

It was hard to stop eating those sourdough flapjacks, and Tommy's stomach wouldn't hold nearly enough of them. He thanked Peg Leg politely for the breakfast and went outside, leaving Chet and Spike swapping friendly insults. The loggers were working high up on Snowside Mountain, the one they just called "The Mountain." They formed a long line as they hurried up the trail to the work site. Snow at the top of the rounded dome of a mountain across the inlet was turning a pastel pink, and a fluffy cloud hung above it—the only cloud in a clear blue sky. The tide was going out, and Tommy walked down to a white sandy beach and tested the water. It was kind of cold, but the sun would warm the sand and the mud flat at low tide, and when the water flowed back over it, they would have a nice swimming beach.

When he returned to the cookhouse, Tommy saw a man with hair as red as his own come out with Chet. He didn't look much older than the bigger kids at school, maybe about eighteen. He wasn't much taller than Chet, but he had great wide shoulders, narrow hips, and pipe-stem legs. He had bright blue eyes, and his sandy eyebrows and the sandy fuzz on his cheeks looked almost white against skin burned brown.

"This is Pinky, the boom man," Chet said. Tommy politely held out a hand, and Pinky took it and held it as if it were an egg and he was afraid of crushing it.

"I'm glad you came up this summer, Tommy," he said. "Maybe you can keep Chet out of my hair. He comes out on the boom and tries to help me, but I spend half my time fishing him out of the drink." He was grinning, so Tommy knew he was just joking.

"Give me another year, and I'll roll you under," Chet boasted. "When I'm grown up, I'll be running my own camp. Maybe I'll make you head boom man."

"Better get started, big shot," Pinky jeered. "When I was your age, I was a darn-good boom man and a crackerjack river driver." He walked out on the hundred-foot boomstick that braced the log raft offshore and called back, "Come out and visit me when you have time, Tommy, but leave Chet ashore. He's kind of a nuisance."

Tommy was afraid Chet would get mad, but he just laughed. "I'm going to sort out Dad's fishing tackle," Chet said. "You might as well look the place over."

Tommy walked along the beach and saw that the long sand spit extended nearly all the way across the inlet and made a three-mile-long lagoon out of the upper end of the arm. A narrow channel along the base of a mountain on the far side connected it with the rest of the inlet. Scrub spruce at the base of the spit shut off the view down the arm, but there were no trees on the outer half of the spit. Tommy guessed he would have a good view from out there.

A narrow valley behind the camp cut a mile-long gash in The Mountain. It was brushy, but a big creek poured out of it. The stream emptied into the lagoon halfway out the spit. Someone had fallen a small tree across it for a bridge. The trunk looked small, but Tommy wanted to cross, so he sat straddling it and hunched his way to the other side. Salmon darted by under him in the shallow water. He saw two big trout with yellow spots on their backs and tails. He considered going back to camp for a fishing rod, but he was more than halfway across, so he went on. There would be plenty of time to fish later.

There were no trees at the far side of the stream, and little bunches of tough wiry grass and tall weeds grew in the beach sand. He could see a long way down the arm. A light breeze blew out of the north. Mountains reflected in the water danced in the ripples. A Nuxalk village was nestled at the mouth of a big river about two miles down the far shore. He saw the unpainted buildings weathered to a dark gray, looking as if they had been there a long time. Tommy figured that Chet's Nuxalk friend Joe must live down there. Maybe he and Chet would row down to see him sometime.

The sun rested like a great golden ball on the round top of The Mountain. Most of the lagoon was now in bright sunlight, and salmon were jumping all over it. He could see a dozen of them in the air at one time, their wet bodies flashing silver-white in the bright light. A big one swam by—Tommy guessed that it was about four feet long—with its fin above the surface in the shallow water close to shore. Chet would really be excited if he hooked a fish that size with light tackle. Tommy thought he would rather start with one of the little cohos he had seen earlier.

A shadow swept by on the water and Tommy looked up. A huge black bird with a white head was diving down from the sky directly toward him. Tommy crouched beside a log and snatched a stick from a pile of wood left by the high tide. He remembered hearing about an eagle that had carried off one of Uncle Phil's lambs. This one looked big enough to fly away with a boy his size.

The eagle came down terrifically fast, but it veered a little and looked as if it would plunge into the lagoon a few yards offshore. Hit at that speed, water would be very hard. It would knock the wind out of a fellow if he belly-flopped into it. But the bird leveled off and shot by with its breast only a few inches above the water. Thick yellow legs reached down below the surface, and the eagle rose, its wings beating heavily. A big salmon was in its talons. The fish looked a lot bigger than the bird. It thrashed violently, swinging its huge tail from side to side. The eagle was thrown off balance a dozen feet above the water. Both bird and fish fell.

Maybe the fish would drag the bird underwater and drown it. Why didn't the fool eagle let go? It could easily get all the small salmon it wanted. An eagle looked awesome when it circled high in the air, but seen at close range, this was an ugly, vicious-looking thing. It righted itself when it was nearly pulled into the water and climbed into the air again. The fight seemed to go on for a long time. The bird would lift the fish a dozen feet above the water, then fall back. Time after time, it looked as if the salmon would surely pull the bird under, but each time, the eagle caught its balance. Tommy lost his fear. If the eagle couldn't whip the fish, Tommy could surely kill the bird with his big stick.

Fish and bird finally dropped heavily on the sand. The eagle struck the salmon several times on the head with its big, hooked beak. Even on the ground and relieved of the weight, the eagle seemed to have trouble getting its talons out of the salmon.

The salmon was beautiful, sparkling in the sun. It would be a shame to let the ugly old eagle have it, so Tommy ran down the beach, screaming and waving his stick. The eagle stood over its prey, big yellow beak wide open, and made hissing sounds like a snake. It looked fierce and scary. Tommy stopped when he saw Chet running up the beach toward him.

"Club him, Tommy," Chet yelled. "He can't hurt you. Club him!"

Tommy wanted to back away, but he couldn't let Chet know he was afraid. He moved a step closer and swung the stick. It wouldn't reach the eagle. But the bird flew up with a thin squeaky squall. So, *that* was the eagle's scream he'd read about. It sounded small and weak coming from such a big bird. The eagle lifted and was only a few feet over him, so Tommy kept swinging the stick at it. Chet threw a stone, and the bird dropped the fish and flew up and up in a tight spiral. The squalls got thinner and thinner.

Tommy's knees felt kind of rubbery, but he seized the fish now lying still on the sand. A big salmon steak would taste mighty good for lunch. Chet offered to carry the fish to camp for him, but this was Tommy's salmon. He'd fought that fierce old eagle for it, and he wasn't giving it up to anyone. "It's a king salmon, and it will weigh in close to thirty pounds," Chet said, but Tommy was sure it was bigger than that. Tommy headed down the beach with the salmon's head over his shoulder and his hands gripping the gills; the tail dragged on the ground behind him. His clothes were wet with slime and scales, but who cared about a little thing like that? Tommy carried his salmon triumphantly back to camp.

It was a wonderful way to start a vacation. And he had three whole months ahead of him. No kid from school would have a better place to spend a summer than South Bentinck.

Chapter 2

A Pesky Porcupine

Talyu Joe was Chet's best friend among the Nuxalk boys from Talyu Village. Joe had explained to Chet that his first name, Talyu, identified him as coming from the Nuxalk territory on South Bentinck Arm. The loggers just called him Joe and so did Chet and Tommy. Joe was a year younger than Chet, nearly as tall but heavier and stronger. Joe was always dressed in overalls and moccasins. He was as brown as a horse chestnut, but of course, the summer sun accounted for part of it. Tommy and Chet were getting quite brown too. Their red hair and hazel eyes made them look even darker. Joe's hair was long and black, his black eyes friendly and mischievous. South Bentinck was his home. Tommy was certain that Joe knew more about the woods, mountains, and wild creatures that lived there than Chet, or probably even their dad.

Joe and Chet were three and four years older than Tommy, but he followed them on their long hikes through the woods. They didn't seem to mind, although Chet grumbled sometimes about having Tommy tag along. Joe never did.

Tommy thought Joe must have telescopic eyes. He saw every little thing around them in the forest and pointed out fascinating birds and animals that Tommy and Chet would have missed. They walked up the little valley behind the camp very early in the morning through heavy brush still wet with the night's dew. A big creek gurgled and splashed beside them.

"Mink passed along here last night," Joe said. "This is Talyu Pete's trapping ground. He will catch mink here next winter."

Tommy couldn't see any tracks on the rocky trail, but he was sure Joe saw them. Then he saw them too, at a muddy place, little round tracks no bigger than dimes. The boys stopped to eat a few salmonberries. There were red and yellow ones on the same bush, both colors soft and juicy, but Tommy liked the yellow ones best because the red berries had kind of a musty taste. Blue grouse hooted continuously on the slopes above the narrow valley. Another birdcall came to them from the creek below. Tommy thought that call was the prettiest song he'd ever heard, so he slipped through the bushes for a look at the singer. He was disappointed. Such a song should have come from a beautiful bird, but the singer was an ordinary-looking, dirty-blue-gray bird. The bird stood on a stone in midstream, rocking back and forth as it sang. The tail feathers weren't completely developed, and they looked as sharp as pins.

"Teeter tail," Joe said. "Pretty song, homely bird."

"It's a spotted sandpiper," Chet corrected him, "but teeter tail is a good name for it. The bird certainly does teeter."

Farther up the trail, Joe pointed out a large brown animal standing in front of a burrow. It looked like a big fat muskrat.

"Mountain beaver," Joe whispered. "He has wide chisel teeth like a beaver, so he can eat roots and woody stems of plants."

"It's a sewellel," Chet said, condescendingly.

Tommy was a little irritated, but Joe didn't seem to mind being contradicted. He just grinned. "Sewellel in books," he said. "Up here, we call it a mountain beaver."

Tommy liked Joe's name for it better than Chet's. It made sense. Soon the animal retreated into its hole, and they moved on.

Minutes later, Joe showed Tommy and Chet an animal that looked like a big rat, but it had ash gray fur and a wide flat tail like a squirrel.

"Pack rat," he said, and grinned at Chet.

Chet grinned back. "It's listed as bushy-tailed wood rat in the museum," he said, "but pack rat is a good name for him. We found a nest under the bunk house with all kinds of shiny things in it: half a box of .22 shells, a tobacco tin, a thimble, and a pair of scissors."

Joe caught Tommy's arm. "Listen," he said. Tommy heard a far-off chattering that sounded like a cage full of monkeys.

"Porky," Joe said. "Come, we'll have a look at him."

They hurried up the trail, and the sound got louder. There was a clicking noise mixed in with it like the sound of ripe wheat waving in the wind. Joe pulled them off the trail, and they crouched behind a currant bush as the sound came closer.

"There must be a dozen of them," Tommy said a little nervously.

Joe shook his head. "Only one. He talks to himself."

An animal the size of a raccoon came around a bend in the trail. It was dark gray, almost black, with a thin white sheen over it. It came toward them slowly, waddling along on short legs and dragging its big tail on the ground. The porcupine was chattering and rattling its quills. Tommy thought it was a silly-looking thing, and it sounded silly too, as if it were carrying on a long-winded conversation all by itself. Its voice had a hundred sounds, and it rose and fell. Its chatter certainly did sound like words. There were periods and commas and question marks in it.

Joe picked up a stick and stepped out in the trail in front of it. The porcupine suddenly got much bigger. Four-inch-long quills stuck out in every direction. He jerked his tail, about eight inches in diameter, from side to side. Tommy expected to see quills flying through the air like a flight of arrows, and he ducked behind a tree.

"What are you scared of, Squirt?" Chet taunted. "The story about a porcupine throwing his quills is so much hooey. He won't lose any of his pins unless you're silly enough to pet him."

Tommy felt a little foolish as he returned to the trail. He watched as the porcupine tucked its nose under its belly, wrapped its long, narrow black hands across its face and rolled up in a ball with quills sticking out in every direction. Well, they looked like hands, but there were no thumbs. Little black eyes peeked out between the fingers, and the chatter became a frightened, angry, scolding sound. Joe poked it with the stick, and the tail slammed against it hard, the quills driven deep into the dry wood. Later, Tommy tried to pull them out, but all the tips were broken off.

"The tips have barbs like fishhooks," Joe explained. "When Talyu Pete's setter puppy got quills in his nose and paw, we had to cut them out with a knife."

"Sometimes a young cougar picks up a few quills," Chet added, "and can't get rid of them. They work in deeper and deeper and eventually the cat dies."

"Most wild things know better than to bother porky," Joe said, "but lynx can kill them. Porky has no quills on his belly. The lynx puts a paw under him like this."

The porcupine's head and paws disappeared completely as Joe pushed a stick under him and yanked it out again. There were no quills in it. Tommy could imagine the cat's long claws tearing at the porcupine's belly, and he felt a little sick. So, even this porcupine has its enemies.

The porcupine was peeking out from between its fingers. "Can we move away and let it alone?" Tommy asked hopefully. "I'm sure it won't bother anyone unless they bother it."

"I ought to kill the destructive pest," Chet grumbled. "It will destroy a lot of timber. The fool game law protects it because it's the only animal a man can catch and kill if he's lost in the woods. I'd have to be very, very hungry before I'd eat one of them."

"Porky tastes good," Joe exclaimed. "Lots of rich fat on him."

"You can have my share," Chet mumbled as they walked around the big pincushion and on up the trail. At the bend, Tommy looked back. The porcupine was still rolled up in a ball.

"He'll stay there half an hour, maybe longer," Joe said. "He thinks we'll hide and wait for him to get up so we can hit him on the head."

They followed the trail up onto higher ground and out of the heavy brush. Now they walked through second-growth cedars nearly as big as telephone poles. Chet pointed to a tree with the bark stripped off one side. Bare, wet wood showed in a strip eight inches wide that went up a dozen feet.

"That pesky porcupine was here," he said angrily. "This damage won't kill the tree, but bark won't grow over the scar, and eventually it will start to rot. When the tree gets big, it will be hollow inside, 'hollow butted' the loggers call it."

"But there are too many trees growing together here," Joe responded. "The stronger ones take sunlight from the weaker ones. Trees like this will die, but the larger trees beside it will grow even bigger."

"Provided the porcupine doesn't come back and strip them when it gets hungry again," Chet argued. "That beast has been working in this grove all spring. You can see a dozen skinned trees from here."

"Porky eats only what he needs," Joe said quietly.

Chet turned away angrily and walked swiftly up the trail. Tommy and Joe followed at a more leisurely pace.

"Chet gets mad, but I don't pay any attention," said Joe with a smile. "Pretty soon, he'll get over it. He likes trees. I like animals."

A quarter mile up the trail they found Chet leaning against a huge cedar. A V-shaped opening on one side led into a round room six feet across. The three of them went inside and found that the hollow tapered up to a point ending a dozen feet above them.

"A porcupine started this probably two or three hundred years ago," Chet began. "The beasts should be exterminated instead of being protected."

Tommy had heard that most big cedars were hollow, and he wasn't convinced that porcupines were responsible for all the damage. But he knew better than to argue with Chet when he was in this mood, so he changed the subject.

"This would be a good place to camp overnight," he said. The foot-deep bed of half-rotted punk wood on the floor had an elusive but not unpleasant smell. He thought it was the stink of rotting wood until he heard Joe's comment.

"A bear slept here last winter," Joe said. "When snow gets deep enough to cover the opening, he has a nice warm house. I'll come up here with Talyu Pete next winter. If the bear comes back, we'll get him."

He picked up a handful of the punk and sifted the powdery stuff through his fingers. "A long time ago before my people had matches, they used this to start their fires. There is not much wood up here dry enough to light with bow and spindle. Porky does some good."

Chet answered quickly. "A hundred years ago, there was plenty of timber and no one to use it. British Columbia was all one big forest. The big trees are getting scarce now. In another few years, there won't be much left that can be logged profitably, so we'll have to start farming our timberland, replanting our trees. We can't afford to feed trees to porcupines."

The porcupine was gone when they went down the trail later in the afternoon. They found him a quarter mile farther down the valley, ten feet up on another small cedar, chewing away at the bark. Chet threw a rock at it, and the porcupine climbed higher, chattering and scolding. It climbed as slowly as it walked, gripping ridges of bark with its hands, and pulling itself up among the branches. Tommy thought a porcupine must live a very lonely life. No forest creature liked it, except maybe another porcupine, and he wondered if even another porky could get very close.

Chapter 3

The Bald-Faced Hornet and The Bulldog Fly

Tommy and Chet lingered over their breakfast of flapjacks and eggs after the last of the loggers had left the table. Spike was elbow deep in suds and dirty dishes; he never sat down at the table for his meals, just kept nibbling all day. He was even skinnier than Chet.

Peg Leg clomped across the kitchen and lowered himself into Dad's chair at the head of the table. His round face and bald head were red and sweaty with heat from the big range. A narrow fringe of gray hair flowed over his ears and low down on the back of his head.

"I enjoyed my breakfast," Tommy said brightly.

"I'm glad somebody liked it," Peg Leg grumbled, but he seemed pleased just the same. The loggers were always in too much of a hurry at breakfast to bother with complimenting the cook.

Peg Leg sandwiched a leftover fried egg between two flapjacks and ate with no show of enthusiasm. "A fellow gets so he can't hardly swallow his own cooking. It's a wonder all cooks don't starve to death."

Tommy tried to look sympathetic, but Peg Leg didn't look starved. He had a big round stomach that Tommy envied a little. A person could stow away a lot of flapjacks in a stomach that size.

"Today's Friday," Peg Leg said, "and I'd like to feed everybody fresh fish for supper. Reckon you kids could catch enough salmon to feed forty hungry timber jacks?"

"We can feed them on fish till they start to grow fins," Chet boasted, but at that moment, he seemed more interested in his flapjacks. A big fly with a shiny green head buzzed around, and Peg Leg swatted it with an empty plate. "Some folks can never learn to close a screen door."

Tommy pushed his plate away. "I'll close it," he said. A spring on the door should have pulled it shut, but one of the loggers had lost a glove and the screen was wedged against it. Tommy laid the glove on a bench so the owner would find it, and the screen slammed shut. Another fly landed on his arm. He swatted it. They were horse flies, but everyone up here called them bulldogs. Their bite could draw blood.

Dad's logging camp on South Bentinck Arm was a wonderful place to spend a summer, but there was one bad thing about it, or rather there were a million of them and all of them had wings. The bulldogs came out on hot days. Swarms of them lived in the woods, but they were worse on the water when anyone was swimming or fishing. But when the sun went down, the bulldogs went to bed. Then the mosquitoes came out. Little black gnats joined them. Joe called them no-see-ums, but everyone could sure feel 'um. Oh, well. No one should expect everything to be perfect.

Chet and Tommy went into their room to get Dad's trolling rod and tackle box. They also needed something to protect them from the pesky insects—flour sacks. They cut holes in them just big enough to let them see and breathe and slipped them over their heads. They put on their coats too, even though it would be hot on the water when the sun got a little higher. A bulldog could bite right through a thin shirt.

Pinky, the boom man, grinned at them as they crossed the log raft to the skiff. "Men from Mars," he yelled. "Don't know for sure, but I think I'd rather be chawed by flies than roasted in one of those outfits."

The hoods were Chet's invention, and he was proud of them. "Your hide is so thick bulldogs can't bite through it," he replied defensively to Pinky. "Maybe after a while we'll grow leather skins too."

Pinky just grinned. He seemed to get a kick out of needling Chet. His skin did look like brown leather. Pinky worked in a thin shirt without sleeves, but the flies didn't seem to bother him.

Tommy took the oars and rowed along the edge of deep water a hundred yards out from the long spit. Chet put a spoon on the line, and it wriggled through the water like an injured fish. They carried a cedar branch in the boat that Chet waved in front of Tommy's face and his own to chase away the flies.

Suddenly, opposite the mouth of the creek, the rod jerked sharply. The reel started clicking.

Both boys ripped the flour sacks from their heads. Chet dropped the branch and pressed down on the reel's leather thumb brake. "A big king!" he shouted. "It feels as big as the one you stole from the eagle." The clicking became a thin whine. Chet leaned back and the line got taut. Tommy was afraid it would break, because it wasn't much thicker than a linen thread, but it was a twenty-seven-pound test line, and Chet knew just how much strain it could stand.

The nine hundred feet of line on the reel had nearly run out when the fish began to slow down. It turned, and when it came back toward the boat, Chet reeled in the line as fast as he could. The salmon passed close to the boat, but it was deep in the water. Tommy saw a flash of silver and it looked awfully big. He was sure he couldn't handle a fish that size, so he was glad his older brother held the rod. Even at this exciting moment, Tommy thought about the little four- and five-pound coho salmon in the lagoon. He wanted to practice by bringing in a small one first.

It seemed as if Chet would never land the salmon. It took one long run after another, but each time, Chet turned the fish until he finally brought it alongside. He slipped the gaff hook into its head and heaved it aboard. The salmon flopped around in the boat. Tommy tried to help by holding down the salmon so Chet could club it, and he was glad it was Chet who'd landed this one. Tommy's overalls and gloves were smeared with blood and slime, but he couldn't worry about a little thing like that.

"Thirty pounds," Chet crowed. "It takes a real fisherman to land one like that. Another one of that size, and we'll have all the fish the crew can eat. All right, Tommy, it's your turn to catch one. If you hook a small one, you can land it. I'll take the rod if you tie into another big one."

They changed places carefully in the skiff, and Chet took the oars. Tommy let out the line. A bulldog landed on his face, and he brushed it away. The glove left a smear of slime under his eye, and before he could wipe it off, the tip of the rod jerked again. A fish leaped high out of the water. It was just a little twelve-inch steelhead trout. Tommy dragged it in disgustedly. "That one doesn't count," he said. "I want a *real* salmon."

Chet must have been feeling mighty good about his big fish, because he didn't protest. "All right," he said. "You can catch three steelhead trout or one salmon, then it will be my turn again." He picked up the oars, then stopped. "What's that?" he whispered, and he sounded scared. Tommy looked in the direction Chet indicated. A black cloud swept toward them. It hung low over the water and kind of shimmered in the bright sunlight. It came fast, and there were little white spots in it. As it swept over the sand spit, it broke up into a million insects, and there was a loud humming sound over the drone of the bulldogs.

"Bald-faced hornets!" Chet screamed. "Sit still, Tommy. Don't even move a muscle. They won't sting us if we sit perfectly still."

Chet sounded scared, and he looked scared. Tommy was frozen with terror. He sat still with his lips pressed tight together and stared straight ahead. He didn't even dare to close his eyes as hornets flew by very close to his face. The droning sound became a thin whine. An explosive roar came from close to his ear. It was like a buzz saw cutting through a knot. A hornet grabbed a bulldog off Tommy's forehead and carried it around in front of him. The hornet was on the fly's back, and their wings beat so fast they were just a shiny blur. The shiny black body looked like two insects joined together by a thread. Two or three inches from his eye, it looked as big as an eagle, and it had a horrible vicious-looking white face. The fly's wings stopped beating and drooped down. It seemed to be dead. The hornet landed on the gunnel and bit into the bulldog. The fly's shell collapsed like a balloon stuck with a pin. The hornet dropped the empty shell and zoomed away to look for another bulldog.

A hornet caught a fly in mid-air and landed on Tommy's knee to eat it.

"The tide is drifting us toward shore," Chet said, and his voice sounded strange because he didn't move his lips. "When we're closer to shore we'll dive in, but don't move until I tell you to."

Through the water Tommy could see the sandy bottom. It looked shallow enough to wade in.

Soon, the fish were nearly hidden under a squirming mass of hornets. The boat seemed full of them! A hundred of them were eating the slime off Tommy's overalls. A hornet landed on his smeared cheek. He tried to keep from blinking, but the wings hit him in the eye, and a muscle twitched. A hot needle stabbed into his cheek, and he was on his feet screaming. Another needle jabbed into his leg. He stepped on the salmon and the crawling mass of hornets. His foot slipped and his knee hit the gunnel hard as he went over the side.

Tommy's hands and knees were on the sandy bottom. He stood up. But when he did, his face was still underwater. The sunlight was close above him and when he jumped, his head popped out of the water. He got a little air in his lungs and saw Chet diving in beside him. But Tommy went underwater again, thrashing around with arms and legs; he kept sinking. He touched bottom and tried to get to his feet again. Then Chet's arm was around him and his head was out of the water.

"Lie still, darn it!" Chet screamed. "Do you want to drown both of us?"

Tommy kept pawing at the water. The boat was very close to him. Chet reached up with one hand and caught the low gunnel, gasping and wheezing.

"What did you want to do a fool thing like that for?" Chet sputtered. "You got me stung on the nose. Hold on, darn it. I'll tow you to where you can stand up."

Tommy realized suddenly that he was in bright sunlight. The shade left by the hornets was gone, but there was a loud buzzing close by. He pulled himself up until he could see over the boat. The swarm was about fifty feet up the lagoon and going away fast. Hornets were zooming up out of the boat and shooting away after the disappearing swarm. Chet held onto the boat with one hand and swam with the other. Tommy tried to paddle too. In a few minutes, Chet was wading. Then Tommy's feet found bottom, and they dragged the boat to the beach.

"Of all the darned fool things to do," Chet growled. "If you'd sat still another minute, we would have been all right."

"I guess you'd have blinked too if you had one of the ugly things in your eye," Tommy said sullenly. "And they were crawling up under my clothes." His voice turned to a wail. "I don't want to fish anymore. I'm going home."

"I guess I can't blame you too much," Chet conceded. "They were scary, but we won't either of us do any more trawling today. You threw Dad's rod overboard, and the reel is heavy enough to sink it."

Tommy remembered having had the rod in his hand when the hornets came. He didn't know what he'd done with it. Maybe he dropped it when he fell overboard.

"It must still be out there" he said. "Maybe we can find it."

The last few hornets flew out of the boat and sped away after the swarm, barely visible way up towards the head of the lagoon. Chet threw the mutilated fish away savagely.

"Let the crabs have it," he muttered. "Peg Leg can serve roast beef for supper."

They found the rod in six feet of water. Chet dove down and brought it up. When the line was dried and the reel oiled, there would be no harm done.

Pinky walked over to them as they tied the skiff at the boom. "You won't need your flour sacks anymore," he grinned. "The hornets gobbled up all the bulldogs."

Tommy had forgotten the hood. He snatched it off the floor of the boat and threw it on the boom logs. Chet tossed his after it. Tommy felt a lot better, even though his knee was sore, and his eye was swollen shut. He'd have a beautiful shiner. Too bad the kids at school couldn't see it. He wouldn't have to tell them how he got it.

"Where did all the hornets come from?" Chet asked. "There must have been a billion of them. The swarm stretched all the way across the water."

Pinky shrugged. "Who knows? They weren't all one swarm. A lot of swarms must have got together. They were migrating. Probably looking for better hunting grounds."

At supper that night, the loggers said the woods had been full of hornets too. A lot of them had stings to prove it. Some of them looked badly shaken.

"When the bulldogs get so bad that men or beasts can hardly live with them, the hornets come along and clean them out," said Big Bill, the hook tender. "Flies will be scarce around here for a few years. Then they'll start building up again. I saw the same thing about ten years ago. It's nature's way of keeping a balance."

"You kids might have got my fish if you'd kept fishing," Peg Leg grumbled. "The hornets weren't coming back after you."

"We'll eat fish next Friday," Chet replied. "I'm going to need a few days to teach Tommy how to swim before he takes a notion to jump overboard again."

Chapter 4

The Bowhead Whale and the Thresher Shark

Only the men who worked near camp ate lunch in the cookhouse. Most of the loggers were working high up on The Mountain. It was Spike's job to haul their midday meal up to them on a stone boat pulled by Satin, a big dun mule. Pinky came in late and slid onto the bench beside Chet.

"There's a billion shiners in the lagoon," he said. "Young herring and candlefish mostly, but there are big schools of half-grown smelt mixed up in them. If you lash your landing net to a long pole, maybe you can dip up enough of them for supper. A mess of smelt would be mighty good."

"Fish," old Dan Harris, the bookkeeper, snorted. "Since you kids came to camp, we've been living on fish. I'm getting fed up with them."

Mister Harris was always grumbling about something. Tommy didn't pay any attention to him. Most of the loggers liked the trout and salmon the boys brought to camp. For those who didn't like fish, there was always plenty of other food on the table. Dad believed in feeding the men on the best there was to be had.

Tommy carried the net lashed to a twenty-foot pike handle when they went out to the log raft after lunch. He was glad to have it to help him keep his balance. They had to cross the hundred-foot-long boomstick that braced the raft offshore, and at high tide the stick tended to roll.

Chet followed with a box to hold the smelt, but he claimed the net as soon as they were on the boom. Tommy gave it up reluctantly. Of course, since Chet had made the net, he was entitled to use it first. Pinky hadn't exaggerated. The lagoon was packed so solidly with the shiny little fish it seemed a wonder they could find room to swim. The net wouldn't pick up the little two-inch herring; they slipped right through the mesh, but they were too small to be of any use anyway. They saw a big school of six-inchers, but they were out a little too far to reach with the net.

"You watch them," Chet said. "If they come in close, call me. I'll see if I can find another school."

Tommy sat down on a big log to stare into the water. Screaming gulls dove down to grab the herring. A school of salmon trout hurried by with their mouths open, scooping up the fish. A rock cod swam out from under the raft. With his big mouth, he could gobble up a quart or more at a bite. A flock of sea pigeons was gorging on them. It seemed that everything swimming in the water or flying over it was preying on the poor little herring. Tommy thought it must be awful to be a herring with everything trying to eat it. They had no way to fight back and couldn't swim fast enough to get away from the bigger fish.

A heavy splash and a popping sound off to the left startled Tommy. He turned toward the noise. Something huge and dark gray was rising slowly out of the water. It came up and up until its back was six or eight feet above the surface. A whale! It was a fearsome thing; it looked to be at least a hundred feet long. Tommy was very close to it. The whale's small black eye seemed to be looking at him. Tommy backed away nervously.

The logs of the raft were packed so closely together they couldn't roll much, and they felt reassuring under his feet, but there was no way of knowing what that monster would do. Chet and Pinky were at the lower end of the boom. Tommy ran toward them, looking back over his shoulder every few steps. The whale lay still in the water, and Tommy slowed to a trot. Chet was looking at him, a disapproving look on his face.

"What's the matter, Squirt?" he called. "He ain't going to climb up on the raft after you."

"He won't hurt you," Pinky added. "Sit down and watch him. He'll put on quite a show for you. Look over there; here come more of them."

Two other whales swam through the channel on the surface, and at least a dozen waited farther down the arm. They didn't look dangerous at that range. Tommy sat down on a big log between Chet and Pinky.

"It's probably the same pod that was in here last summer," Pinky said. "They stuck around nearly a month, and they got to be a nuisance. They came up among the loose logs so close to me sometimes I could have jumped on their backs, but I didn't. Didn't know if they'd like having a fellow walking around on them in caulked boots."

"Here comes the biggest one!" Chet shouted. "Watch him."

The whale came toward them, parallel to the raft and about twenty feet from it. It came fast with just a little of its back out of the water. It slowed down and stopped when it was almost directly in front of them. It came up slowly and made that popping sound again. It was like somebody pulling a cork out of a bottle. A thin spray shot up from the top of the whale's head, and it smelled awful. Tommy was getting nervous again. But Chet and Pinky didn't seem scared, and they knew all about whales, so it must be all right, he told himself.

The little black eye was visible again, and once more, it seemed to be looking directly at Tommy. The eye seemed to twinkle at him, and somehow, the monster looked kind of friendly now, even though its jaws must have been twenty feet long. Hundreds of little herring stuck out from between his lips. A dozen screaming gulls swooped down, and their wings slapped against the whale's face as they picked fish out of his mouth. The dark eye was still twinkling, and Tommy decided that the whale must not object to having the birds steal his food.

"He swam through the herring with his huge mouth wide open, and there's a ton of herring in his gullet," Pinky explained. "The few the gulls get won't amount to anything. The birds are his friends; they often guide him to food. He watches them, and when they start feeding, he rushes in and gobbles up the hog's share."

The whale, with its back eye still on Timmy, slowly drifted past them with its enormous mouth wide open. Tommy could see its large white lower lip that was turned up as if in a friendly greeting. Tommy noticed the big tail was crosswise instead of up and down like a fishtail. The small flukes looked like elevator fins on an airplane. They started working up and down and the whale surged ahead. Soon, his head went down out of sight, and then the massive body was gone. Only a little white foam was left on the surface, marking the spot where the great whale had disappeared, but the excitement wasn't over, because five or ten more of the giant creatures were charging around the lagoon, scooping up a ton of herring at a bite.

"It's a wonder any of the herring ever live to grow up," Chet mumbled.

Pinky shrugged. "Every female herring lays a million eggs, and most of them hatch," he said. "There'll always be plenty of herring. Wow! Look at that cow and calf."

The calf was probably a dozen feet long, but it looked tiny beside the big cow. She rolled over on her side, and Tommy could see half her grayish-yellow belly. There were big rolls of fat on it, separated by narrow bands of tight muscle. It looked like the old-fashioned washboard the loggers used to scrub their clothes. The calf had a teat in its mouth and was sucking greedily.

Chet pointed at something to the right, and Tommy turned. It was like trying to watch a three-ring circus. Something was rising out of the water a hundred yards away. There were two of them, like big logs standing on end, rising slowly until there was a dozen feet showing above the surface of the water, about eight feet apart. They leaned together at the top, and Tommy could see a triangle of sunlit water between them. They gradually closed together at the bottom and rose higher. Tommy realized it was a whale's head!

"I've seen them rise up like that before," Pinky said. "I could never figure out what kind of hinge a whale has in its jaw." In the middle of the lagoon, a whale came up with a rush that lifted more than half its length out of the water before it toppled over and came down with a heavy splash.

The whales must have eaten all they could hold. Most of them just floated on the lagoon. They looked almost black in the bright light.

Pinky rolled a cigarette. "The loggers are moving a donkey engine up on The Mountain this afternoon, so I haven't much to do," he said. "I suppose I should go ashore and bore boomsticks, but I always feel lazy on a Saturday afternoon. How would you fellows like to go up Asachie Creek with me tomorrow and spear some big steelhead trout? I know where the Nuxalk keep their spears, and they won't care if we use them."

Tommy was more interested in the whales. The biggest one floated lazily to the surface very close to them. Water and a thousand small fish cascaded down off its back.

"I wouldn't have believed any living thing could get so big," Tommy said.

"The bowhead is the second biggest mammal in the world," replied Chet. "Only the sulfur-bottom whale is bigger. They get to be 120 feet long and weigh 150 tons. We don't see them up here."

"Chet is a walking encyclopedia of useless information," Pinky said to Tommy, grinning. It was a good description of Chet. He knew a little something about everything and liked to show off how smart he was.

"No information is useless so long as you get your facts straight," Chet said loftily. He was probably right, but watching bowheads was a lot more exciting than listening to a lecture on sulfur bottoms.

Then, before Tommy could respond to what his brother had said, the biggest whale dove, and he was down a long time. When he came up, he had an octopus in his mouth. The tentacles waved around the whale's big head like snakes as he drew them into his mouth with a chewing motion.

Another whale raced by and bit the ends off some of the tentacles before he could swallow them, and she slapped him with her flukes as she went by. That blow would have killed an elephant, but the big one paid no attention to it and placidly continued to chew the octopus.

Pinky got up and stretched. "We'd better go in and wash up for supper," he said.

Tommy was surprised. It didn't seem possible for the afternoon to be gone so soon, but the sun had already dropped down behind the mountains to the west, and the shadow was creeping up the slope across the inlet. Time always seemed to slip away too fast when he had something exciting to see or to do.

Pinky and Chet walked along the raft, and Tommy followed reluctantly. At the end of the boomstick bridge, he paused for one more look at the whales.

"What's that?" he shouted. Something long and slender rose out of the water and stood straight up. It was twenty-five or thirty feet long, and looked like a telephone pole, but it moved over the surface swiftly. The big whale came to the surface beside it, and the thing slammed down across his head like a falling tree.

"Thresher!" Pinky yelled. "Head for the shore. We'll have scared whales charging all over the lagoon!" He and Chet ran along the boomstick. Tommy wasn't sure what the excitement was all about, but he ran too.

"It's a thresher shark," Pinky said when they were on the beach. "It swims beside a whale while they are both underwater, and when the whale has to come up for air, the thresher slams it over the head with its tail. If it can hit directly over the blowhole before the whale gets fresh air in its lungs, the thresher will drown it."

"There is a thresher shark in the museum at Victoria," Dad said during supper that evening. "You boys had better fly over there some weekend and have a look at it. After seeing this one you'd find the trip well worthwhile. The thing has a shark's head, a short, very thick body, and a thirty-foot-long tail. It's an ugly-looking brute that will scare you just to look at it."

After dinner, Tommy and Chet returned to the lagoon. They saw the thresher and the big whale again in the deep dusk of the evening, way up near the head of the lagoon. There were no other whales in sight; they all must have found their way through the channel and gone back toward the inlet.

There were no whales in sight when Pinky rowed toward the head of the lagoon early the next morning. Tommy sat in the stern beside Chet and looked around a little anxiously. He didn't want to meet the old thresher out here in a small skiff, but the thing had probably gone away by this time.

There were fifty or sixty acres of marsh grass at the head of the lagoon. It was underwater at high tide, but the tide was very low now. There was a hundred-yard-wide mud flat between the grass and the water. Asachie Creek fanned out over it and wouldn't be more than an inch deep. They couldn't drag the skiff into it, so Pinky headed toward the mountains to the west and beached the boat on a steep rocky shore.

A narrow finger of water extended back six or eight hundred feet between mountains and marsh grass at half-tide. It was dry now too. They crossed the mouth of it, and Tommy saw the whale. It lay on the mud at the head of the inlet.

"It's dead," Tommy wailed. "That mean thresher killed it."

"It swam up in here to get away from the shark," Chet answered. "Let's have a look. I never saw a whale out of water."

Chet and Pinky ran toward the whale. Tommy followed slowly. He wanted to see the stranded whale, but he was a little frightened too. He had seen dead animals and fish, but death in such a big creature seemed much worse. Because the inlet narrowed at the tip, the whale had gone as far as it could on high tide. It lay in a trough a little narrower than its big body. It had looked enormous in the water, but it seemed even bigger now. From the bank where he was standing, Tommy figured the whale's back was six or eight feet above his head, and it was a full hundred feet long. Tommy didn't want to get too close to it, but Chet laid a hand on its dark gray side. The great mass seemed to quiver, and he leaped back from it. Pinky laughed.

"It ain't going to bite you," he said. "It ain't going to live too long either. A whale can't swim backwards. If it struggles at high tide, it will just wedge itself in tighter."

The big tail lay flat on the mud. Occasionally, it raised a few inches and fell back with a loud, slapping sound. Tommy's fear was replaced by concern. He walked close to the whale's head. The black eye looked much too small for such a big mammal. It was glazed like frosted black glass, and it seemed to look at him pleadingly.

"Can't we do something for him?" Tommy asked miserably. "We can't just stand around and let him die."

"Just pick him up and carry him out to the water, Tommy," Chet said sarcastically. "He only weighs about eighty tons."

Pinky scratched his red stubble of whiskers thoughtfully. "There's a hundred feet of light line in the boat," he said. "If we can get a bite around his fluke, maybe we can drag him down to open water at high tide, provided he doesn't struggle. If he does, there won't be a thing we can do for him."

Tommy hurried to the boat and returned with the coil of line, and they laid it out on the mud, making a big loop with both ends toward the open water.

Pinky found a sharp stick and tried to dig a trench under the fluke. It raised a few inches again. Chet jerked the bite of the line under it before it fell back, plastering the three of them with mud.

"That's what we get for trying to help you," Pinky sputtered. "We ought to leave you here to rot, you big tub of blubber. Only if we did, you'd stink up the whole lagoon."

Tommy was too excited to mind a little mud or Pinky's disrespectful words. He watched the tide creep up the inlet to the whale and beyond it. It would have to rise another dozen feet or more before the whale would float. Pinky sat down on a log and rolled a cigarette.

"There's nothing to do but wait. It's a nineteen-foot tide. High at one ten."

"How long can a whale live out of water?" Tommy asked anxiously.

Pinky shook his head. "I don't rightly know. They breathe air like any other animal, but there's an awful lot of weight pressing against his stomach and lungs. One got wedged in between my boom and the shore when I was down in Simoon Sound. There was a wire cable between my boom and a stump on shore, and he got it in his mouth. He couldn't back up, and there wasn't room for him to turn around. He stayed there for two tides. We had to get rid of him because he was right in front of the camp, and we couldn't have lived with that much rotting flesh so close to us. I got a line on him, and we towed the creature out into deep water on the second day. He was too weak to struggle by that time, but surprisingly, that whale recovered and was in the sound all summer."

This one would have only been aground twelve hours come high tide. He'd surely live if they could get him out into deep water. Tommy watched the tide creep slowly up the dark gray sides of the whale. It was funny how fast the tide came in when you wanted to swim in shallow water on the sun-warmed flats, and how slow it could be when you waited for it to float a stranded whale.

But the tide came in, the five-foot-deep trough was full, and water was spreading out through the marsh grass. There was still a whole lot of whale above the surface but every inch of water around him was probably taking nearly a ton of weight off his underside. Tommy could see the big sides heaving as the whale drew air deep into his lungs.

"He came in here on a twenty-one-foot tide last night. Maybe he won't float on this tide if he came in at the top of the flood," Pinky said.

"If we can't get him off today, I'm coming down here tonight," Tommy replied. "There'll be a full moon. Of course, I know he might be dead by that time."

He walked up beside the whale's head. The eye on this side seemed a lot brighter. Probably the one on the other side was too, by this time. Maybe he was gaining strength too fast.

"Let's have lunch," Chet called. "There won't be time to eat after he floats."

They ate the lunch Peg Leg put up for them, and for once, Tommy didn't notice what he was eating. Chet said they should have gone fishing for the steelhead trout while they waited, and Tommy was a little irritated. How could someone think about fishing when the whale they were trying to help might be dying. Tommy was growing fond of the old whale.

Pinky looked at his watch. "Eleven thirty," he said. "High tide in forty minutes. I think he'll float. There isn't much more of him out of the water than there was yesterday when he was floating."

The rising tide still flowed into the narrow inlet, but it had slowed down a lot. The incoming tide brought the water nearly up to the trees, and there wasn't much beach left. It was time for action. Pinky tightened the lines and held a steady strain on them. Tommy pulled on them too, and the whale seemed to move a tiny bit. Chet caught the lines behind Tommy, and the whale moved a little more.

"When he takes a big breath there isn't much weight on the bottom," Pinky whispered. "Just keep a steady strain on him, and don't make any noise that might startle him."

The huge body moved a foot and stuck again for a minute; then it moved steadily, but very slowly, against the current. When the ebb tide started, the whale would drift out of the inlet. They had only to guide it and keep it in the deepest part of the channel.

Pinky let go of the line and stood beside the whale, pushing offshore with a long pole. Tommy moved down the beach and once the heavy whale gained momentum, it moved easily. The flukes lay still in the water, and the ebb was beginning. Tommy had to trot to keep the line tight.

Western hemlock and yellow cedar leaned out over the water. In some places, Tommy was wading knee deep to get around them. A million candle-fish swam down the channel. They brushed against the whale and against

Tommy's overalls. Tommy, Chet, Pinky, and the whale were nearly to the mouth of the inlet and the tide was getting stronger.

The whale floated faster down the channel, but soon its big flukes began to move, and that moved the whale back toward the beach against the outgoing tide. Tommy sat down hard in two inches of water and the lines were jerked out of his hands, but Chet held on. Tommy scrambled to his feet and caught the lines again.

They still were moving down the beach. If the fool thing would lie still just a few minutes longer, it would be all right. They were at the skiff, but the whale was facing the inlet. If it swam now, it would go right back into it. Whales were rigid, and they couldn't turn sharply as a fish could. Tommy held a strain on the lines, and Chet moved the boat out of the way. Pinky joined Tommy, and they pulled the tail in close to shore. The tide was swinging the whale's body around slowly.

The whale was headed toward the big mud flat. If it swam now, it would go aground again, but at least it was out of the inlet and would drift offshore on tonight's tide. Of course, it might be dead by that time. Tommy held his breath. Pinky tied one end of the line to a tree, and they held a strain on the other end. The big tail was so close to shore they could almost touch it, and the body was swinging around. It was headed toward open water when the flukes moved again. It jerked the line out of their hands and the whale moved offshore a few feet.

Pinky coiled the line in the boat, and they watched breathlessly as the tide drifted the whale out into the lagoon. The flukes moved again, a little more feebly, and the whale slid further toward deep water.

"I throw little ones like that back," Chet grinned. "I'm after big fish."

"So long, blubber boy," Pinky yelled. "I hope you get back in fighting trim before you meet that thresher again."

But it wasn't a joke to Tommy. It was a very weak old whale, but it was swimming steadily now, slowly, moving under its own power.

Pinky put an arm across Tommy's shoulder. "It will be all right," he said. "Makes a person feel good to think he could rescue anything the size of that old bowhead. Here comes his harem."

The cow and calf were swimming into the lagoon. Another big whale surfaced up by the camp, and the gulls swooped down on it. More whales rushed around the lagoon, scooping up the minnows. The whole pod was back, so the thresher must have gone someplace else to find a victim. *Well, Tommy thought, this will be a great story to tell the kids at school this fall. Certainly, none of them ever saved the life of a hundred-foot whale.*

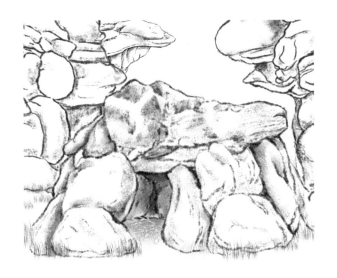

Chapter 5

Talyu Joe

Days were long at South Bentinck in late June. You could read a book out-doors at ten o'clock at night, and probably at two in the morning, if you stayed up that late. But days were never long enough to suit Tommy. Dad's logging camp was a wonderful place to spend a vacation. The sky above the big mountains was a pastel pink, and the lagoon seemed to glow as Tommy sat in the stern of the skiff and Chet rowed it toward the head of the inlet.

The tide was high, and the big marsh-grass meadow at the mouth of Asachie Creek was under water; just the tips of the six-foot-tall plants were above the surface. The creek flowed down the middle of the valley and turned sharply near the edge of the grass flat, then east six or eight hundred feet parallel to the beach. Another turn and then it flowed into the lagoon. The current wasn't strong, and Chet rowed against it quite easily. Soon they saw a split-cedar cabin at the edge of the forest. Joe stood before it, waving at them.

People seldom used his full name, except the silly Nuxalk girls sometimes when they wanted to tease him. The loggers called him Talyu Joe. Joe was all the name Tommy needed for him, and Joe liked it better that way.

"Why is Joe staying up here all by himself?" Tommy asked.

"He is watching for the candlefish run to start," Chet answered. "When the fish come in, he will go down to the village to alert the Nuxalk people."

Tommy had never seen a candlefish, but he knew it was a rich, oily fish. Joe had described it as longer than a young herring with white markings like a smelt. The Nuxalk buried boxes of them in the ground to rot out the oil that they used for butter and gravy, dipping their bread and meat in it. The loggers called the fish "hooligans," and the oil, "hun grease." They spoke of it contemptuously because they thought the Nuxalk way of drawing out the oil was unsanitary, but it was perfectly clean when it was strained. Tommy had eaten some of it the day he and Chet had lunch with Joe's village, and it tasted good.

Joe's canoe was tied to a stake driven deep into the clay, and Chet beached the skiff beside it.

"Any candlefish yet?" Chet asked as they scrambled ashore.

Joe shook his head. "Just a little school early this morning. The big run will come tomorrow or maybe the next day. We have time for a walk up the trail."

Tommy followed the bigger boys up the old trail, through bushes wet with dew. Water dripped from huge spruce, cedar, and cottonwood. Mosquitos were bad in the early morning, but they didn't seem to bother Joe, and they would disappear when the sun rose above the mountains. The day would be hot, but it would be pleasant in the shady forest.

Asachie Creek gurgled and splashed beside them. Little humpback salmon hurried through the riffles. They were almost black with splashes of red on their sides, and some of them had big humps just behind the head. Tommy had seen humpies at the markets in Vancouver. They were as bright and as streamlined as any of the salmon.

"These fish are ripe for spawning," Chet explained. "The males get the humps when they get near fresh water."

Joe stopped at a deep pool and showed Tommy a dozen little ten-inch fish. They were shaped like trout, but they had bright blue backs and white bellies. "Candlefish," he said. "When the big run comes, we catch them in nets. Mighty good eating."

"Can we catch them on flies?" Tommy asked eagerly.

Joe shook his head. "Candlefish don't eat in fresh water. They lay eggs and go away. Next year they'll come back."

"We don't know yet where the candlefish goes when it leaves the creeks," Chet said. "No one has ever caught one in salt water. It probably goes out in the ocean and stays deep where a net won't reach it, and they won't take a bait. The fishery department has tagged a lot of them, so we know they always come back to spawn in the creek where they were born."

"When salmon spawn, they die," Joe added. "Candlefish and Dolly Varden trout spawn and go away. Next year, they come back and lay more eggs."

They went onward, and Joe showed Tommy a little yellow animal about eight inches long, and no bigger around than a thumb. It had a long furry tail and very short legs. "Weasel," he said.

"I thought weasels were white. Isn't that where we get ermine fur?" Tommy asked.

"He is wearing his summer coat," Joe explained. "White in winter, yellow in summer."

It seemed that Joe knew all there was to know about the creatures of the forest and streams, and Tommy was learning a lot from him.

The creek forked. A big stream poured out of a narrow gorge to the east. A smaller and more sluggish one flowed down the wide valley. The trail followed close beside it. The trail up hadn't been used much lately, and in some places it was hard to follow, but Joe knew every foot of it.

A loud splashing sound came from up stream. To Tommy, it sounded like a salmon going over a riffle, but Joe motioned them to be quiet, his eyes shining with excitement. He slipped through the bushes to a big windfall. Chet and Tommy followed him and peeked over the tree trunk. A big black bear stood belly deep in the water with one forepaw held above the surface. Two cubs stood on the bank across the stream, cute little fellows about as big as raccoons. Tommy thought they would make nice pets, but the mother bear looked big and dangerous. She was kind of scary. He had seen bears before at a distance, but this one was barely twenty yards away.

"She won't hurt us if we don't get too close to the cubs," Joe whispered.

The mother bear's paw plunged underwater in a scooping movement and hurled a salmon out onto the bank. The cubs seized the little humpy and had it half eaten before it stopped wiggling. They growled and slapped at each other with their forepaws, each trying to get more than its share of the fish. They were as greedy as some of the kids at Hastings Academy.

Mother bear scooped out another salmon but then raised her head, sniffing the air. She scrambled up the bank, looking kind of clumsy but moving fast, making little grunting growls while the cubs slipped out of sight into ferns. She seized the salmon and disappeared in ferns and bushes, which didn't look nearly high enough to hide such a big animal.

Joe stood up. "She smells us," he said regretfully. "Black bears are timid. But don't get so close to the *mesachie* bear. Mesachie is fierce and dangerous."

Joe must mean the grizzly bear or the big yellow cinnamon, Tommy thought. *Dad said they weren't really dangerous if you didn't get too close to them. He told us that we must always talk or whistle when we are in thick brush so the bear can hear us in time to get out of our way.*

Further up the trail, Tommy heard a drumming sound. There were three slow, booming beats, then a lot of them in quick succession like a roll on a snare drum. It came from no particular direction—or from every direction—and it was repeated every three or four minutes.

"Willow grouse," Joe said. "I like to watch them."

They slipped off the trail through heavy brush that got lower and thinner as they worked back from the creek. On higher ground, they were at the edge of a stand of hemlock trees, and Joe led the boys up behind a cluster of hazel.

The drumming came again, and it was much louder. Tommy peeked through the tops of the bushes and watched as a big brown bird strutted along a fallen tree. He thought it must be a partridge, but its feathers were fluffed out, so it looked three times as big as the partridge he had seen in Stanley Park in Vancouver. The black ring around its neck was puffed out in a big ruff. The black-tipped tail feathers were fanned out in a half circle. The wings were held away from its body and drooped down a little.

The bird turned and walked slowly back to a spot where the bark had been worn smooth. Its wings raised and came down against the log three times, making hollow, booming sounds; then they moved so fast the eye couldn't follow the movement. Tommy wondered how they could move so fast without lifting the bird off the log.

"It's mating season," Joe whispered. "He's calling for the lady grouse."

Tommy hoped the girl would come. It was such a pretty bird, and the male grouse had been calling to her for a long time. The bird walked along the log about thirty feet, then turned back toward the worn spot.

"He must have been using that tree to send out his love calls for years," Chet said. "Air trapped under the wings makes the booming sounds."

Chet was right, of course. He knew about things like that, but just the same, Tommy could see that the wings did strike the log because the bark was worn smooth.

Joe caught Tommy's arm. "Look," he whispered. A little brown head rose up from behind the tree. It was too big for a squirrel. The animal rose higher, and Tommy saw bright orange fur on its neck and chest.

"Marten," Joe whispered. The small animal came up on the log. The light brown head was nearly as long as the body, and the creature had very short legs. The bird couldn't see it over its fanned-out tail and the marten darted toward it in a hump-backed gallop.

Tommy was on his feet quickly, screaming, "Look out, partridge!" The bird flew away with the loud roar of swiftly beating wings. The marten turned its head and seemed to be glaring directly at Tommy out of little black eyes. The squall it made seemed much too big for such a small animal.

"The marten lost his dinner. He doesn't like you, Tommy," Joe grinned.

"I don't care if he doesn't. The partridge will like me, and he's a beautiful bird."

"The proper name is ruffed grouse," Chet said. "Up here, it's called willow grouse. Other places, it's partridge or native pheasant. I never saw one drumming before, and he certainly was beautiful."

They walked on up the trail and over a great pile of boulders. Sometime, probably a long time ago, a section had broken loose from a granite precipice that seemed to reach all the way up to the sky. It blocked the half-mile-wide valley, and a good-sized lake had formed behind it. Near the head of the lake, they lay down in the grass to rest.

It was nice up there in the warm sunshine. The grass was soft and warm. Chet was talking to Joe about a big trout he had caught up here last summer. Tommy listened drowsily for a moment, then closed his eyes. He dreamed of ancient peoples resting in this very place.

Joe woke him suddenly from his reverie. "Look, here comes shitepoke," he said, pointing towards the sky.

Tommy shook his head to make sure he was awake and looked to where Joe was pointing. There it was: a blue heron. It came up the lake on big floppy wings and landed on the shore very close to them. It looked extremely tall with its long legs, long body, long neck, and long beak. Its back was a dull blue. Long feathers in mottled reds and grays hung down from its chest like the bibs Aunt Martha used to put on Cousin Judy when she was a baby.

They lay still, and the heron didn't see them. It looked as if it were walking on stilts as it waded out in the lake. When it stopped, there were two birds, one upside down in the water. It stood still a long time, turning its head to look down in the water with one eye, then with the other. Finally, the head darted into the water and came up again with an eight-inch trout in its beak. It waded ashore and dropped the flopping fish on the grass. The bird managed to get the head in its beak and swallowed the fish whole. Tommy could see the bulge slide down its long, skinny neck. One fish seemed to be all it wanted, and it flew up and landed on the branch of a dead tree by the shore.

"Some people want to kill all shitepoke because they eat too many fish," Joe explained, "but they only eat what they need. Fish were theirs before Thunder Bird brought the first peoples to the coast. We can share, and I like to watch them."

They went on, crossing a cranberry marsh at the head of the lake and then into a forest of Douglas fir with huge limbs high overhead. The limbs were so thick the sunlight couldn't peek through them. The valley ended where another valley crossed it like the top of a T. A big river of milky glacier water poured down it from the east and emptied into another lake.

"Someday, if your father lets you stay out overnight, we will go down to that lake," Joe promised. "It's a beautiful lake. We can't go that far today, but come, I'll show you my stone house."

When they saw Joe's house, Chet and Tommy realized that it had not been built by human hands. Rocks had fallen into the valley from a cliff maybe thousands of years ago. A huge block had landed on top of other blocks, leaving a dry space with a narrow opening. This space formed Joe's stone house: a room, rather dark because of the narrow opening, but large enough to create a comfortable living space. Joe had dragged in cedar boughs, and they sat on them as they ate the lunches Peg Leg had packed for them.

"I stayed up here alone for three months when I ran a trapline last winter," Joe said.

"Don't you go to school?" Tommy asked.

Joe shook his head. "I went to school in Bella Bella for five years, but I'd rather trap."

"Pretty soft," Tommy said. "I wish I could quit school and go trapping." He looked around the shelter then and realized that staying alone in the stone house might not be such a good idea. He'd probably be scared if he had to stay up here alone, especially at night.

They went outside and Tommy noticed four poles lying on the ground in the form of a cross with the ends about a foot apart. There were ashes between them. Joe examined it carefully. "Wuikinuxv people have camped here, three, maybe four weeks ago, a big party."

Chet nodded. "The fire was made since the last rain, but a lot of dew has fallen on it. How do you know Wuikinuxv people made it?"

"None of the people from my village come up here," Joe said. "And it's a Wuikinuxv people fire. White men make a big fire, roast on one side, freeze on the other. We make a small fire, lay close to it, and keep warm all over. When the fire dies down, we move the ends of the poles closer together and the fire flares up again. But these people have moved up the river, probably looking for good trapping grounds. They saw my traps, so they won't come back."

Tommy looked around nervously, and Joe laughed. "Nuxalk people don't fight Wuikinuxv people anymore. The last battle was a long time ago when my grandfather was a little boy. Come. It's better we go back. Candlefish might come in on the night tide. I must go and get people from my village."

Tommy followed the bigger boys back down the trail. He was a little tired, but it had been a wonderful day, and there would be a lot more of them before he had to go back to the boarding school.

Chapter 6

The Bald Eagle and the Mountain Goat

It was a beautiful little lake, about three miles up the valley above the head of South Bentinck Arm. Chet said there were a lot of big trout in it, but if the fish were there, they weren't rising to the fly. It was a good chance to practice fly casting anyway. That last one was almost as good as Chet could do. Tommy retrieved the fly and heaved it back over his head, stripping off a little line from the reel and jerking the rod upright. The slender tip jerked forward, and the brown tackle sailed out twenty feet over the lake. It fluttered down lightly on the water. Nothing happened, but he wasn't expecting a strike, so he wasn't disappointed.

The middle of a hot summer day was the poorest possible time for fly-fishing. The trout were all lying on the bottom in shady spots. A fellow might hook one on salmon eggs or worms, but Chet said it was too easy to take trout on anything but flies. Tommy twitched the tip of the rod two or three times to make the fly dance. It didn't look like any real fly he'd ever seen. A fish would have to be really dumb to think there would be a real fly with a big brown body and scarlet wings. The fool things did strike at them though in the evenings or early mornings.

The lake was right up against mountains on the east side of the valley. There were big Douglas firs and alders with white trunks and shiny green leaves on the far side. The reflection in the water was brighter than the trees themselves. Behind the narrow belt of forest, a granite cliff went up and up till it touched a sky that looked like blue steel.

A big brown duck with yellow bill and legs waddled out of the high grass at the head of the lake and swam a few feet offshore. She quacked softly and a dozen fluffy little yellow ducklings swam out to her. Two of the little fellows climbed up on their mother's back for a ride. An old mallard was very close to Tommy before the hen saw him, and she flopped away along the surface. The ducklings fanned out behind her, flapping their little bony, featherless wings. They moved amazingly fast.

Tommy's fly had sunk to the bottom. He felt a little pull on it. If the thing was a trout, it must be a very small one. He reeled in and dragged a waterdog out on the grass meadow. Of course, the little yellow-bellied lizard was harmless, but he hated to touch it. He put a foot on it lightly to pin it down while he loosened the hook and the lizard flopped back in the water.

Fishing for trout that wouldn't bite wasn't Tommy's idea of sport. He leaned his rod against a big Douglas fir and stretched out in the shady grass under it. Chet was fishing a hundred yards down the shore. He wasn't catching anything either, but it was nice up here even if the fish wouldn't bite. Tommy rested lazily on his back. A bird was drifting around in circles high against the sky. It was probably an eagle, and it must be nearly as high as the mountaintops. It would be wonderful if a fellow could float around in the air like that. He could land on the tip of a high mountain and could probably see halfway to Vancouver from up there. That might not be so good though. The snow and glaciers looked very cold.

There were white spots high up on the granite precipice, and they seemed to be moving. Dad's binoculars lay on the lunch box. It was too much trouble to get up. Tommy rolled over twice, and he could reach them. He adjusted the glasses and a huge billy goat seemed to leap at him off the cliff. It moved along slowly and was looking right at him. The thing was as big as a bear. He hadn't dreamed a goat could get so big. It seemed to walk on the wall like a fly. There must be a narrow ledge up there, but looking up, he couldn't see it.

The goat stopped and reared up on its hind legs with its fore feet against the wall. Something green grew out of a crack two or three feet above it. The goat leaped up and grabbed the thing in its mouth, and Tommy held his breath as it slid down onto the ledge again. It slowly lowered itself to all fours and stood munching its tidbit and looking at Tommy. The big ham seemed to be waiting for applause like a performer on the high wire at a circus.

Chet was coming down the narrow strip of grassy meadow along the shore. He leaned his rod against the tree alongside Tommy's. "It's no use," he said. "They won't bite until the sun works around behind the mountains. Let's see what Peg Leg gave us for lunch."

Peg Leg generally put a surprise in the lunch box he prepared for the boys. This time it was blueberry tarts.

"He must have got up early this morning to bake them for us," Tommy said. "There were none on the table for dinner last night. We mustn't forget to thank him." He wanted to sample one, but Chet said he had to eat the sandwiches and hard-boiled eggs first.

They sat in the shade with their backs against a rock, and Tommy peeled an egg. He tossed the bits of shell on the ground and three birds about the size of meadow larks swooped down on them. "Canada jay," Chet said. "Up here, they call them whiskey jacks or camp robbers. Keep the lunch box covered, or they'll get your tarts."

The birds were gray with white breasts. They dropped the bits of shell and their scolding chirps sounded angry. Two of them flew up in a tree, but one stood very close to Tommy's foot. It tilted its head and stared at him out of a shiny but dark little eye. Tommy tossed it a piece of egg yolk and the other two swooped down to quarrel with him for the morsel. Tommy scattered a handful of breadcrumbs in the grass and more of the birds appeared from nowhere. They were so tame they'd almost snatch food out of his hand.

Chet held a sandwich in one hand and a telescope he'd borrowed from Pinky in the other. He was watching the goats high up on the wall.

"Look at the nanny with the two kids," he said. "Cute little guys."

Tommy focused the binoculars on the big billy. It was lying down under a rock overhang. To the right and lower down, a nanny walked along a ledge that sloped downward sharply. The kids followed close behind her. The ledge ended at an angle in the wall where a huge boulder had broken loose at some time, maybe long ago, and tumbled down into the valley. The nanny leaped six or eight feet across the break, seemed to brush the cliff with a forefoot, turned at a right angle, and leaped again onto a wide terrace a dozen feet lower.

There must have been a rock projection up there big enough for one foot to land on, but from the valley, the cliff looked perfectly smooth. One of the kids followed her but the other backed away along the ledge. It made two or three false starts but stopped before it reached the end of the ledge and backed away. Tommy couldn't hear any sound, but the nanny's mouth was open. He imagined she was blatting encouragement. The little fellow appeared to be afraid of the jump, but maybe more afraid of being left alone where its mother couldn't get back to help. Tommy held his breath as the kid made a running leap. It seemed to cling to the wall a long moment with a half mile of thin air under it, then it leaped again down onto the terrace, and the old nanny began licking its face like the cows on Uncle Phil's farm licked their calves.

Tommy let out his breath explosively. "The little guy's got more courage than I have," he said. "I wouldn't even dare to stand way up there on one of those ledges."

"I don't know as I'd care to try it either," Chet said. But his tone implied that of course he could do it if he had to.

Something touched Tommy's knee. A camp robber ran up his leg to snatch a crumb from his sandwich. It darted away but the sandwich fell on the ground. Tommy sat perfectly still, and the birds darted in to peck at it. He could have reached down and touched the sandwich, but they rushed in to grab a mouthful and flutter away with it. They flew away suddenly, and Chet was on his feet shouting.

"A bug hatch! Grab your rod, Tommy."

The water seemed to be boiling about twenty feet offshore, and Chet was running toward it. Tommy grabbed his rod and ran too, and the birds fluttered down on the sandwich.

Trout backs and fins were swirling around in the disturbed water. The water from the bottom of the lake rose in little mounds and flies burst out of them into the air. Chet was hooked up to a trout, and Tommy dropped his lure directly onto the boil. There was a swirl and his reel was singing. Chet's fish ran straight offshore, but Tommy's took off toward the head of the lake and he ran along the shore to follow it, keeping a tight line, but of course, he couldn't put much strain on a trout leader.

It was an awfully big trout, much bigger than any he'd ever caught. He tried to remember all the things Chet had told him and wished desperately that Chet was beside him to remind him what to do. He could only hold on and hope the fish would tire before it took out all his line. There wasn't much left on the reel.

The trout turned and leaped out of the water about a hundred feet offshore; it was the biggest rainbow Tommy had ever seen. He could see the broad crimson stripe on its side glimmering in the bright sunshine. The spindle of his reel looked about as big around as a lead pencil. There couldn't be more than a dozen feet of line left on it.

Chet had landed his fish and was casting again. Tommy's big rainbow leaped, but it wasn't so far offshore this time. Chet had hooked another one that ran offshore too. Tommy was afraid their lines would cross and get tangled. Chet would be cross if they did. He reeled in fast to get his fish out of Chet's way. Chet's fish leaped, and Tommy saw scarlet on its throat. A freshwater cutthroat. It wasn't as big as Tommy's rainbow.

The water here was shallow close to shore. Wild rice grew in it. The rainbow trout was just beyond it. Tommy could see it through reddish-brown water. It was as big as a humpback salmon, but he couldn't coax it in closer. It was off on another run. Chet worked down the shore and tossed the net into the grass to Tommy.

"Land your fish and bring me the net," he shouted, but he was facing away from Tommy. All Tommy could remember of Chet's instruction was not to keep too much strain on his tackle and take in line when the fish would let him. The thing seemed to go on fighting forever, but the runs were getting shorter, and Tommy was gaining confidence. He couldn't coax the fish into the rice, but he waded out to the edge of it. The trout lay still in the water on its side. He led it in slowly and finally slipped the net under it. Tommy floundered out of the water onto shore with the trout flopping in the net. It was nearly two feet long. Surely it was the prettiest, biggest trout anyone had ever seen. Chet was yelling for the net. Tommy hit the rainbow on the head with a club to stop it flopping and took the net up the Chet.

"Nice one," Chet said, "It's bigger than mine. You did fine, Tommy. I'll make a fisherman out of you yet."

Tommy ran back to loosen the hook from his fish. Chet's first one lay in the grass, another cutthroat about fifteen inches long. It looked small beside the big rainbow. The water had stopped boiling and there were no more flies. A thin oil slick was all that was left. He tried a few casts, but the trout seemed to have gone away.

Chet came back with an eighteen-inch trout and examined Tommy's rainbow. "Nearly five pounds," he said, "Bigger than most of the ones I've caught."

"Where did the bugs come from?" Tommy asked. "They seemed to fly right up out of the water."

"They did," Chet said. "A fly lays its eggs in the lake. They sink down into the mud and seem to all hatch at once."

"The things can't fly when their wings are wet," Tommy protested.

Chet scratched his head a little puzzled, but he came up with an answer. He always did. Maybe they weren't always the right answers, but they always sounded plausible.

"They are covered with oil when they are first hatched," he said, "so they don't get wet." It sounded kind of reasonable, and there certainly was a little oil on the water.

The trout had quit biting as suddenly as they had started. After a few more casts, Chet and Tommy went back to finish their lunch. Tommy bit into a tart. It was delicious. The whisky jacks swooped down again, and Tommy grinned at them.

"You don't get any of this," he said. "We've only got one apiece, and we can't spare a crumb of them."

Chet nibbled a tart and focused the telescope on the rock wall. "Look!" he screamed.

Tommy crammed the last of the tart in his mouth and picked up the binoculars. The nanny and the two kids were walking along a narrow ledge, and a huge black bird with a white head swooped down the face of the cliff toward them. It came terrifically fast. Tommy tried to scream a warning, but it came out a strangling gasp.

The eagle's thick, yellow legs shot out, and its great hooked talons struck the nanny just behind the shoulder. Bird and goat locked together, tumbled from the ledge. The nanny's legs were moving as if she were running in midair. Animal and bird turned over slowly two or three times before the eagle could loosen its hold, following her down in a tight spiral. It was like something seen in a nightmare. The goat seemed to fall very slowly. She hit a ledge and bounced off it.

Tommy watched through a film of tears. He couldn't lower the binoculars or turn his eyes away, but he was glad the nanny was hidden behind the trees across the lake before she hit the rocks at the foot of the cliff. It seemed to be a long time before he heard a sickening thud.

"The poor little kids," he wailed. "What will they do? They'll starve to death."

The kids huddled closer together on a ledge, looking down. The big billy was on his feet and watching the nanny and eagle too. Chet's arm was around Tommy.

"I'm sorry you saw that, Tommy," he said, and his voice sounded shaky too. "You'll just have to get used to things like that. It happens all the time in the woods and on the mountains. Wolves and coyotes kill the deer. Birds kill insects. Martins kill birds. Big fish eat little ones. It's nature's way of balancing the books. If some of the game weren't killed, there would soon be so many deer and goats there wouldn't be enough food. They would all starve. I don't know why it has to be like that. We'll just have to accept it."

"But I wish we could catch the little fellows and take them to camp," Tommy sobbed. "They look so little and helpless."

"I do too," Chet said. "But there's no way we could get up there to catch them. They'll be all right. Another nanny will find them and adopt them."

"I don't want to fish anymore," Tommy said. "I'm going home."

"I guess I've had enough for today too," Chet said.

They walked back down the trail. Tommy carried the big rainbow, but his pride in it was gone. He was a killer too. People were as bad as eagles and wolves. They all killed so they could eat.

Chapter 7

A Mean Old Otter

Joe's stone house was warm and cozy from the small fire burning at the entrance. Since Tommy was only ten years old, he could stand up in the room that had been formed by boulders falling from a cliff high above. But Chet and Joe were three and four years older, and they had to stoop to keep from bumping their heads. Yes, there were some advantages to being small, but not many; most of the time, the older boys had all the best of it.

Tommy lay on blankets spread over a deep, springy bed of cedar boughs at the back of the room. He watched the fire growing brighter in the deepening darkness. This was his first camping-out trip, but he wasn't afraid. Maybe he would be if he were alone, but with Joe on one side of him and big brother Chet on the other, he felt safe. The supper of mountain trout the boys had shared felt warm and comforting in his stomach.

Dad hadn't liked the idea of letting Tommy and Chet stay out overnight in the mountains, but when he learned that Joe would be with them, he decided it would be all right.

This was Joe's way of life. First Nations people had been living like this for thousands of years. Lying there in the darkness, Tommy thought that it would be nice to be a Nuxalk boy with no school to go to, nothing to do but fish and swim, hunt, and trap. Maybe not so now, but in the old days, that must have been what it was like. And he realized then that one of the best things about this summer at Dad's logging camp was having Joe for a friend.

Joe and Chet were talking, and Tommy listened drowsily. "I found a new otter slide when I fished downriver," Joe said. "Mama otter and maybe eight or ten little otters use it. The little otters will be big this winter and then I can trap them."

"I'd like to see otters playing on their slide," Chet said. "If we go there tomorrow, will the otters be there?"

"Maybe, but early in the morning, I want to show you beaver people at work. There's a big colony living about two miles downriver."

Tommy wanted to watch the otters playing on their slide too, but more than that, he wanted to see the beavers. Of course, they weren't people, but Joe respected the beavers as he would wise men, and he was eager for Tommy and Chet to meet them. The fire slowly died down, and the ruby red ashes looked like eyes staring mysteriously at him out of the darkness. Now the voices of Joe and Chet were just a drone, and the words didn't mean anything. Still, it was nice to know that they were there beside him.

In the early morning darkness, they ate breakfast by the light of the campfire. Tommy was too sleepy to know what he ate. Chet was muttering something about animals being so wild a person had to sneak up on them in the dark.

"Beaver people work early in the morning," Joe said. "They have warm coats, and they go to bed when the sun comes up."

Trees and bushes were just beginning to take shape as Tommy followed Joe and Chet down the trail. The forest looked mysterious and kind of scary. Almost anything might be lurking out there in the darkness. The long, lonely howl of a timber wolf drifted down from somewhere up on The Mountain. Band-tailed pigeons cooed drowsily near the top of a tall fir. Little creatures rustled in the low bushes, and a white owl floated by silently. The bird looked big, ghostly, and kind of scary.

The trail turned away from the river and climbed to higher ground. Joe pointed. "Beaver pond is over there, so now we'll go downstream about half a mile. I built a bridge when I trapped here last winter."

Tommy could see something big and dark across the river. There was black water behind it covered by a thin, silvery sheen. From up here, the sawtooth peaks to the east stood out sharply with a narrow band of pearl pink over them.

Joe left the trail and led them down a rocky slope through bushes wet with dew. Tommy was soaked to the hide, and his teeth were chattering a little. As usual, Joe didn't wear a shirt, but if he was cold, he didn't say anything about it.

Below them the river gurgled and splashed. It sent back peals of booming laughter where it poured into a narrow canyon. Tommy saw Joe's bridge, a tree cut down so it spanned the canyon. Joe walked across. Chet followed him. He seemed to sway dangerously. Tommy decided to crawl across on his hands and knees, but he still felt dizzy when he looked down at the tumbling water twenty feet below. Joe laughed at him, but Chet said it was the right thing to do.

"When you are not sure of yourself, don't take any silly chances," he said. Tommy knew that Chet would have crawled across too if Joe hadn't been there. He couldn't resist doing anything Joe did. Chet was a little jealous because Joe was a better woodsman. But then again, Tommy thought, Chet was learning a lot from Joe and so was he. After a couple more summers with their dad at the logging camp, they would be great woodsmen too.

The morning became brighter as the sun rose, and they worked their way back upstream on a deer trail. A thin mist hung over the river, and just a hint of a breeze blew downstream.

"It's good," Joe said. "The beaver people won't catch our scent."

Tommy caught sight of the dam through a cluster of willows. It was a big mud wall with the ends of limbs sticking out all over it. It must have been more than a hundred feet long at the top. Deer and bear had made a trail across it. The river swirled along its base about thirty feet below.

"I never dreamed it would be so big," Chet marveled. "It must have taken the beavers years to build it."

Joe nodded. "Beaver people have been here a long time. They work now at the upper end of the pond."

The pond was a quarter mile long and about half as wide. It looked like quicksilver in the morning light. Joe slipped silently through low bushes and ferns, walking in a low crouch. Chet and Tommy followed, doing their best to imitate his movement through the brush. Halfway along the shore, he raised his head to peek through the tops of bushes and then pointed at something on the far shore.

"Beaver *illahee*," he whispered. Tommy saw two round-topped mounds made of sticks and mud. Beaver houses looked like gigantic beehives, mostly on shore but with the edges in the lake. The entrances must have been underwater. A big, brown head bobbed to the surface, and a beaver swam toward the head of the lake. Close by, a small stream tumbled down off The Mountain, probably a big creek in rainy season, but now it was just a trickle. The lake was low now too, and there was a narrow strip of grassy meadow around it.

Joe motioned to them to be quiet, then turned and slipped silently toward the head of the lake. Where bushes were low, he dropped to hands and knees to crawl. Once more, Chet and Tommy followed and moved as he did. There was a stand of very big alders up ahead about a hundred feet back from the shore, and Tommy heard an unfamiliar sound coming from that direction. It reminded Tommy of the lambs bleating on Uncle Phil's farm.

The sound became louder as they crawled up behind a big clump of hazelnut bushes and peered through the top branches. There was a ditch, three or four feet wide from the lake to the alders. Tommy thought that the beavers must have dug it, and it must have taken them a long time.

Raising his head a little higher, Tommy saw the beavers. Two of them stood upright beside a big alder, balancing themselves with wide, flat, leathery-looking tails. They were round and chubby, and their fur was light brown. Tommy later learned that this was their summer color. On land, they looked much bigger than they had in the water—they stood more than two feet tall. They were calling to each other as they used their wide chisel teeth to gnaw thin chips from a big alder, spitting out the wood as they worked and chatted.

On the side of a tree facing the lake, the beavers had cut a big notch. It would serve the same purpose as the undercuts loggers at the camp made to guide a tree's fall. Another cut at the back of the alder was higher and shallow at the sides.

The tree was about twenty inches in diameter, and the beavers were working behind it. Tommy heard a faint crack of breaking wood. Then another. The beavers kept on gnawing out chips until there was a much louder crack. Like expert loggers, they moved back and dropped to the ground, standing on their wide flippers. The cracking became continuous. The tree leaned with a loud rustle of wind in the branches, then crashed down, landing with a heavy thud, parallel to the ditch and two or three feet from it. Fallers at the logging camp couldn't have done a better job of it.

Beavers popped up in the water by their domed houses. More came out of the woods across the pond, and Tommy noticed the entrance to another canal over there. A dozen more swam toward the fallen tree. They waddled across the meadow on their flippers. It was kind of a clumsy gait, but they moved fast, much faster than seals could on shore.

They chewed off the limbs and trimmed them, eating the leaves and twigs. Some of them started cutting the trunk into lengths small enough to be rolled into the ditch. They worked like the buckers and limbers at the camp. Maybe Joe was right in thinking of beavers as people. *Or people as beavers*, Tommy thought.

A beaver started across the lake towing a trimmed branch. When it was a few feet offshore it stopped, raised its flat tail out of the water, and slapped it down on the surface making a sound like the crack of a rifle shot. Suddenly, all the beavers moved toward the canal. Those close to the water dove into it. In a moment they had all disappeared.

"They see us or smell us," Joe said regretfully. "It's better we go. The beavers won't come back today."

"I don't get it," Chet said. "What did they want the tree for? They didn't eat the wood."

"Beavers eat only the bark," Joe explained. "They bury limbs and small pieces in mud at the bottom of the pond, so they will have food when the freeze-up comes in winter. In summer they eat bark from big logs."

The boys found a little ditch that extended across the tangle of brush. There was a half-finished dam of clay and twigs across it.

"Young beavers have been playing at making a dam," Joe grinned. "Wish we had seen them. Cute little fellows no bigger than a setter puppy." He stopped and gazed out over the lake. In the distance, beavers were appearing, and they all swam toward the dam. Some of them towed peeled branches. Three big ones raced out ahead of the others. The boys were in plain sight, but the beavers paid no attention to them. Joe caught Tommy's arm.

"Look!" he said excitedly. "Otter. The beavers didn't see us. They saw an otter. Come, quick. We'll see a big fight."

Tommy saw a long, brown animal with short legs. It was on the dam, tugging at a limb. Joe turned off into the brush and raced toward it with Chet at his heels. Tommy ran after them doing his best to keep up.

Soon they slowed down and worked their way up behind a cluster of willows where they could see the water. Since it was midsummer, the water was a foot or more below the top of the dam. But the otter had torn a hole in the dam below the surface and water flowed straight through it. The otter's slender body was about five feet long. It looked something like an overgrown mink but the tail, about eighteen inches long, was triangular like a big three-cornered file. Its short legs were bunched together and its back arched high in the air. It was tugging and jerking on a limb and soon pulled it out of the clay that was getting wet and soft. The flow of water through the break got bigger.

The three big beavers were trying to pull themselves up on the dam. *They'll tear the otter to pieces with their wide chisel teeth if they catch him,* Tommy thought. But the otter didn't run away. It leaped toward the nearest beaver, and there was something snake-like in its head when it struck. Tommy saw blood on the beaver's cheek. The otter was everywhere, striking at any head it could reach. The lake was turning crimson, and water rushed through the break in the dam, washing away mud and sticks.

"Help them," Tommy implored in a quavering voice. "The otter will kill them."

Joe pulled him down behind the willows. "Quiet," he whispered. "You'll scare the beavers, and their dam will be destroyed."

A dozen beavers were trying to pull themselves out onto the dam. The otter darted at one, then another. Soon, deep crimson gashes appeared in their cheeks. Two beavers came out of bushes across the pond and moved out on the dam, side by side. The otter rushed toward them but stopped. Other beavers had pulled themselves out behind him, and they closed in on him from both sides. The otter whirled and leaped over them, far out over the river. It turned in a graceful arc and struck the water head-first with its front paws under its chin. There was hardly a splash and only a little foam to mark the place where it vanished in the milky glacier water.

The enemy was gone. But the damage was done. Water rushed through the hole in the dam, and the break got bigger by the minute. Every beaver in the colony must have been close by now. Only the big males were in the fight to save the dam. Females and yearlings were towing poles and branches. Eight or ten yearlings each towed a small limb.

"What will they do if they lose the dam?" Chet asked. "It would take them years to build it up again."

"Quiet," Joe whispered. "They'll fix it."

The beavers worked quietly, methodically. No specific one of them seemed to take charge of the operation. They were like a well-drilled team; each knew its assignment and swiftly carried it out without fuss or excitement.

Two big males floated a pole across the break and sank it down under the surface. Then moved out of the way while another pair set another one. The water pressure held the logs in place. The flow slowed to a trickle. Two beavers were in the break and others dragged limbs to them. They sank the sticks into the wet clay. There was no pattern to it, but each limb locked the last one firmly in place.

Half the females were diving to the bottom and coming up with a quart or more of the wet clay hugged against their bodies with a front flipper. Beavers on the dam took it from them and pushed it down in the hole. The two old engineers pressed it tightly around the limbs. The young beavers were on the bank, cutting down bushes and dropping them in the water. A big female gathered up the bushes and passed them on to the dam. Most of the females and yearlings were racing back up the lake, looking for more big limbs. The hole was filling up and the flow of water stopped, but the wet clay looked like a flimsy barrier.

One beaver was looking suspiciously at the clump of willows where the boys were hiding. "Come on," Joe whispered, "we must go away and let the beaver people finish their job." The boys wriggled away on their stomachs, and when they stood up, the pond and the dam were hidden behind bushes.

"Why did the otter do it?" Chet asked. "He didn't want to eat the beaver, did he?"

"Otters are like some men," Joe said angrily. "He just likes to make trouble for others. I will catch him with a trap next winter and get twenty dollars for him, maybe twenty-five."

"Will you trap the beavers too?" Tommy asked, a little fearfully.

Joe shook his head. "There is no open season on beavers now. Not many beavers are left."

They worked back along the hillside across the river, and Tommy saw the dam again. It looked a lot bigger from over here. The sun was high and hot. The wet clay glistened in the bright light. Most of the beavers had vanished. Two big ones lay on the dam to stand guard until the clay dried and set firmly.

Tommy followed Joe and Chet back to the stone house, a little hungry after the hasty breakfast, but happy. It was nice to know the beaver people would be in their pond when he and Chet came up here again next summer. Surely, they were the wisest animals in the world. He wanted very much to watch them work again.

Chapter 8

Old Barnacle Back

"Hey!" Tommy yelled. "Two of them, big ones. Come a running!"

The two Dungeness crabs were about the same size. They appeared to be about a foot across the back, but of course, things seen through six feet of clear water always looked bigger than they really were. One of them had a light grayish-brown shell; it lay still about twenty feet from the old abandoned logging trestle at the head of South Bentinck Arm. The other had a very dark brown shell with two big barnacles on its back. It was moving slowly out from under the trestle.

Ties on the trestle were spaced about a foot apart. A person had to be careful when walking on them, so Chet couldn't walk very fast, but he seemed to be taking all day getting out to where Tommy waited. Tommy thought he must still be annoyed because the ebbing tide had left the skiff high and dry on the beach, and Tommy felt a little guilty about letting it go aground. But Chet didn't have to be so cross about it; he made mistakes too.

Chet carried a crab rake. It was his own design, and he was very proud of it. Shucks! It was just an old garden rake he'd found in the logging camp tool shed. Chet had woven a wire basket from the ends of the rake to the handle and lashed it to an eighteen-foot pike pole. It wasn't much of an invention. Nothing to be so proud of. It worked fine, though. Chet could pull the rake under a crab and turn it over. The crab would be helpless on its back in the basket or have its legs tangled in the wire mesh. But Old Barnacle Back was so far out that Chet couldn't reach it when he finally joined Tommy on the trestle.

"If you hadn't let the boat go aground, I could easily get both of them," he grumbled. "Can't I trust you to ever do anything right?"

"How did I know the tide would go out so fast," Tommy asked irritably. "I wasn't gone but a minute, well … not more than four or five. I saw a big buck and slipped up to the edge of the brush for a better look at it."

"Deer," Chet snorted. "We see deer every day. It's nothing to get excited about."

"Not like this one," Tommy said. "It was the biggest and prettiest deer I ever saw. It had wide, curved horns with five points on each side, and they were matched perfectly."

"You get so excited you don't know what you see," Chet sneered. "I have never seen a buck bigger than a three pointer with evenly matched antlers. It probably had five points on one side and four or six on the other."

Tommy watched the crabs in sullen silence. Just because he was fourteen, Chet thought he knew everything. The buck *did* have evenly matched horns. It was a beautiful deer, and just because Tommy was younger didn't mean he was so dumb he couldn't count five points.

"Here comes Old Barnacle Back," Chet said excitedly. He sounded as if he were over being mad. Chet never stayed angry for very long.

The big crab came toward them slowly. It walked sideways, moving its eight legs one at a time, the needle-pointed tips sinking deeply into the sand. Its big white claws were folded across its chest, or across where its chest would be if a crab had a chest. It found a little piece of seaweed and reached out with a claw to pick it up like a person would pick up something with his hand and put it in his mouth. Tommy could see its mouth plates shuttling apart and together again, and the weed disappeared. The crab lay still a long time. Gray Shell was half-buried in the sand, and he didn't move.

"They've got their bellies full and are curled up for the day," Tommy said pessimistically, "if a crab's got a stomach."

"Sure he has," Chet said out of the superior knowledge of his extra four years. "It's under the back of the shell. That yellow custardy stuff we wash out of a cooked crab is half-digested food."

Chet was probably right, but the information didn't seem very important. Tommy sat on the trestle with his chubby legs dangling between the ties. Watching two crabs that wouldn't come close enough to get themselves caught wasn't his idea of excitement. The tide was still falling, and the mud flat between their boat and the water was more than a hundred feet wide. Two boys couldn't possibly drag the heavy skiff over that sticky clay. He should have watched it better while Chet was up on The Mountain with Dad's camera trying to get a picture of the area. If Chet had stayed on the beach, Tommy could have had a picture of the big buck. That would prove the horns were evenly matched.

From the trestle, Tommy could see a long way down the arm. The narrow inlet was so pretty with its high, snow-capped mountains on either side. Salmon were leaping everywhere, those at a distance appearing as silver flashes in the bright sunlight. Two miles down the shore, he could see the logging camp. Too bad they hadn't brought a lunch along today. It would take an hour to walk to camp over the mountain trails, and then they would have to come back for the stranded boat. It would be a shame to waste two hours out of the middle of a warm summer day. Vacation wouldn't last forever. One of those big crabs would make a lunch for both of them. Of course, two would be even better. Barnacle Back moved a little closer to the trestle and stopped again.

"He's the one I want," Chet whispered. "But I'll take Gray Shell too if I can get him."

"They look to be about the same size to me," Tommy countered. "What difference does it make?"

"The gray one shed its shell not long ago," Chet explained. To Tommy, he sounded like a teacher at school trying to explain something to a dumb kid.

"He isn't a soft shell, but his meat would be kind of watery. The legs and claws wouldn't be very well filled out. Old Barnacle Back is a regular old hard shell. His meat would be firm and sweet."

"How can you tell?" Tommy asked, as if he didn't quite believe what his older brother was saying.

"By the color," Chet answered. "The darker the color, the harder the shell. Anybody should know that. Old Barnacle Back has worn that shell a long time. If he hadn't, the barnacles wouldn't have grown so big."

"That makes sense," Tommy admitted. There were barnacles on most of the crabs he had seen, but there were none on Gray Shell.

Barnacle Back was moving again, but this time parallel to the trestle just out of reach of the rake. He moved slowly, stopping from time to time, not going anywhere in particular and in no hurry to get there. His tiny black eyes on the ends of feelers more than an inch long could look straight ahead or to one side or to both sides at once. Barnacle Back seemed to be looking at the gray crab. After stopping for a moment, he moved toward Gray Shell.

Gray Shell's legs came up out of the sand, and he backed away. The crabs could walk backward or forward, but when they ran, they moved sideways. Gray Shell backed toward the trestle and was nearly close enough to reach with the rake.

"Just a little closer," Chet pleaded, "just two or three feet closer."

Gray Shell darted off to the right, but Barnacle Back headed him off. They stood facing each other with their claws spread like the arms of wrestlers trying for a hold.

"They are going to fight," Tommy said, sounding a little alarmed.

Chet grinned. "What are you worried about? Let them fight; they can't hurt each other very much. Gray Shell will be no match for Old Barnacle Back. He might lose a leg or two, but if he does, he'll grow new ones."

Tommy had seen a crab with one little leg starting to grow out where it had lost one. Too bad people and other animals weren't like that. It would be wonderful for Peg Leg.

The crabs circled each other, and Barnacle Back moved in, closer and closer. They circled with their claws extended, ready to strike. Gray Shell seemed to know he was no match for this more heavily armored adversary, and he kept trying to run away but was always headed off. At times they were almost within reach of Chet's rake, but at the last moment they moved away again.

The fight ended suddenly, dramatically. Tommy thought it must be like that when a prizefighter was knocked out in the ring. Barnacle Back's right claw reached out and grabbed the gray crab's shell between the eyes. There was nothing to prevent Gray Shell from getting the same hold, but it seemed to be instantly paralyzed. Its legs moved feebly a moment, then Gray Shell lay still.

"There must be a brain or nerve center in there," Chet observed. "But I've examined cooked crabs, and I never found anything that looked like a brain."

Barnacle Back kept its hold and worked around Gray Shell. Its other claw reached down under the gray crab and caught something, probably a mouth plate. He lifted the shell up and the back plate rose like the lid of a box. The legs moved feebly, and then Gray Shell lay still. Barnacle Back lowered the shell onto the sand, dipped his face in the partly digested food, and tilted back with the mouth plates moving very slowly as if he were eating dessert and wanted to make it last as long as possible.

"The dammed old cannibal," Chet sputtered. "I've never seen anything like that before."

Tommy felt sick. In the last few days, he'd seen dead crabs on the bottom with their back shells lying upside down beside them and had wondered what killed them. Now he knew: Barnacle Back must have been acting crazy here for days, killing every gray crab he could find.

Barnacle Back dipped his mouth in Gray Shell again and tilted back. Its mouth plates continued to shuttle open and shut slowly. The crab seemed to be looking directly at Tommy with kind of a leer on his face. Tommy thought he might be saying, "I'm going to eat Gray Shell, but you won't be able to eat me, because I won't come close enough for you to catch me."

"Maybe it sounds silly to talk about expression on a crab's face," Tommy muttered, "but it's there. He seems to be laughing at us."

"Yeah, it seems silly," Chet agreed, "but the way the mouth and eyes are placed does create a face with an unpleasant expression. I can't figure out how he gets that effect unless it's the movement of the mouth plates. That's the only thing on a crab's face that can change."

A little red rock crab moved out from under the trestle. It wasn't more than four inches across the back. The legs were very thin, but it had huge claws and its shell was so hard it would take a hammer to crack it. Barnacle Back stopped eating to watch the approaching rock crab. He spread his claws threateningly, but the little crab kept coming. Barnacle Back left his feast to edge away from it.

The rock crab put its mouth into the food Barnacle Back had abandoned, then moved around the dead crab to face the larger crab. Both had their claws extended and Barnacle Back made threatening rushes toward his smaller opponent but always stopped before he was in range of the small crab's huge claws.

"A cruiser against a battleship," Chet grinned. "The little fellow has the heavier armor and the bigger guns, and Old Barnacle Back knows it."

Barnacle Back wouldn't lower his dignity by running. He moved backward toward the trestle and seemed to be saying, "Don't think you're scaring anybody. I've had all I want to eat, so I'm giving you Gray Shell."

The handle of the rake seemed to bend at a sharp angle when Chet lowered it into the water. It was hard to judge just where it would hit bottom, but Chet had the move worked out to perfection. He reached over Barnacle Back, dragged the rake under him and flipped him over. The old cannibal lay on his back in the basket with his legs thrashing helplessly.

A small fire burned on the beach. A five-gallon can half full of salt water hung over it, and the water was just coming to a rolling boil. Chet picked up the big crab, gripping the hind legs close to the body with his hand turned so the back of it was toward the crab's back. There was no way the big pincers could reach him.

"If you're too squeamish to watch me execute a murder, turn your back," Chet warned.

Just as Tommy turned his back, he heard a little splash. He quickly turned around and saw the crab's legs hit against the rim of the pail. Then the only movement was that of the boiling water. Barnacle Back lay still with his legs and claws folded tightly against his body. Tommy wondered who the murderer was, Barnacle Back or Chet. Maybe they were equally guilty. They both killed so they could eat. He remembered the eagle and the nanny goat, and it came to him again: Everything was like that—people, animals, and fish.

Tommy felt a little sad, but it didn't affect his appetite. He ate his share of the crab with enthusiasm, much like what he had witnessed when Old Barnacle Back had made a meal of Gray Shell.

Chapter 9

A Lovable Old Bandit

Tommy, Chet, and Talyu Joe walked along the shore in the early morning. The channel into the big lagoon at the head of the arm was narrow, even at low tide. Most of the mountains to the west across the lagoon were in bright sunshine, but the logging camp buildings near the beach were still in deep shade. There wasn't even a hint of a breeze, and the smooth lagoon looked like a big mirror. Tommy wondered why scenes reflected in the water always seemed more brightly colored than the objects they reflected.

It was really pretty up here. Tommy hated to think of the time when he and Chet would have to leave the logging camp and go back to Hastings Academy. But, he thought, there would be no sense in spoiling a lovely morning by thinking of that now. There was more than a month left of their vacation.

A tall snipe ran along the beach before them on ridiculously long legs, so long that it reminded Tommy of a bird on stilts. Soon it flew out over the lagoon, circled back, then landed behind them and continued its interrupted breakfast.

A duck with a very long, very narrow red bill flopped out across the lagoon from the mouth of a small stream and a dozen fluffy little yellow ducklings followed her one after the other in perfect formation. There were always fascinating things to see and to do. Days were long in late July, but they were never long enough to suit Tommy.

Chet ran along the beach and leaped across the stream, but Tommy and Joe liked the feel of cold water on their bare feet. They waded across, laughing and splashing. Although Joe was thirteen, nearly as old as Chet and three years older than Tommy, he liked to do all the things Tommy liked. No kid ever had a better companion.

A narrow, hard-packed game trail angled up the slope to a tangle of salal brush. Joe stopped to examine it. "A big raccoon went along here," he whispered. "He's not far off. Maybe we can get a look at him."

At Joe's mention of a big raccoon, Chet grumbled. "Well, if there's a raccoon around, he isn't more than two minutes ahead of us, but you two made enough noise back there to scare him out of the province. We will never see him."

"He won't run," Joe replied firmly. "He'll walk slow. Probably we'll find him at the clam beach."

Tommy couldn't see any tracks on the hard ground, but Joe pointed to a damp spot. When Tommy moved just a little, the light was at a different angle, and he saw the wet print of a little hand. It was long and narrow with four fingers and no thumb.

They walked quietly along the slope above a narrow belt of salal, and soon the trail took them up onto a high, rocky point. Beyond that was a small horseshoe-shaped cove, its gravel bottom bare at low tide. Tommy remembered the time when they had dug clams in the cove and roasted them in a campfire. This was the place where big clams called cockles could usually be seen on top of the gravel. They were nearly as big as baseballs, but only Joe liked to eat them. Chet and Tommy didn't like the tough texture and strong taste of cockles; they preferred the smaller littleneck clams that could be found just a few inches under the surface. The littleneck clam's meat was tender and the flavor delicate.

At the base of the point, they stood in high bushes and looked down at the cove. The raccoon wasn't in sight, but they saw a raven rise with a cockle in its beak. The clam was heavy, and the bird rose steeply with wings beating hard.

"Watch him," Joe said. "He'll drop the clam on a rock to break the shell."

There was only one large rock in the cove, a nearly two-feet-wide black one with a round top near the water's edge. The bird kept climbing until Tommy guessed it was about a hundred feet above the cove.

"He will be a good shot if he can hit the rock at that distance," Chet remarked.

The raven maneuvered clumsily for a minute or so, then dropped the cockle. It seemed to fall slowly, and the bird followed it down halfway to the ground, then rose again with an angry croaking squawk.

Joe caught Tommy's arm and pointed. A raccoon the size of a bear cub and nearly as clumsy was running toward the rock. It seemed to run hard but didn't move very fast. Its big bushy tail with black and gray rings was nearly dragging on the ground. A black stripe across its eyes looked like a Halloween mask.

Tommy heard a sharp crack as the cockle landed squarely on the rock and rolled down onto the gravel. "Bullseye," Chet laughed. "That overgrown crow must have a bombsight. Maybe he should join the air force."

The raccoon stood over the cockle and looked up at the raven. He seemed to be laughing at the bird. The raven croaked again and flew away to look for breakfast some place where there wouldn't be so much interference.

The raccoon sat upright with a flexible black hand curled around the undamaged side of the shell. With the other, he picked off bits of broken shell. Then he took the cockle to the water and washed off all the sand and shell fragments. The hands seemed almost human as the raccoon picked the meat out of the shell. Finally, he gnawed the tough muscle off the shell and headed back to the salal brush and disappeared.

"That's the biggest raccoon I ever saw," Chet said. "He must weigh forty pounds."

"He's a big fellow," Joe agreed. "Next winter I'll catch him in a trap."

Tommy felt a little sick. It was a nice old raccoon, even if it did steal the raven's breakfast. He would have enjoyed having the big furry fellow for a pet.

"They travel a lot," Chet said. "By next winter it may be a hundred miles away.

Now Tommy felt a little better. "Let's dig some clams and roast them," he suggested.

"You just got through eating about forty of Peg Leg's flapjacks," Chet teased. "Don't you ever get enough to eat?"

It was a big lie, of course. Tommy was sure he hadn't eaten forty flapjacks or even half that many. Chet ate more than he did, but he didn't say anything because it was too nice a morning to waste time quarreling with Chet

"Let's go up to the falls," Joe suggested. "Catch trout. Then we can have a fish fry when Tommy's belly is not so full."

They agreed. The beach ahead was steep and rocky, so they walked along an open slope above the salal. The mountains and most of the lagoon were now in bright sunshine. Salmon were leaping in the lagoon, so many that the boys could see half a dozen of them in the air at the same time. But one of them rose more slowly, tail first and thrashing as if it were trying to swim. They could see nearly all of it by the time a seal's head broke water, the salmon's head in its mouth.

"Everything preys on the salmon," Tommy observed sadly. "It's a wonder any of them get back up the stream to spawn."

"Your people kill more salmon than they can eat," Joe countered. "The seal takes only what he needs, nothing more."

"A hair seal is no good to anybody," Chet grumbled. "They should be exterminated. There is no sense in letting them kill valuable fish."

"Seals are good, a part of our lives," Joe told him. It was an old argument that had been going on for weeks. Neither Joe nor Chet could ever accept the other's point of view. Chet wanted to conserve only things that were valuable to people. Joe loved all living things. He killed animals for food or skins, but like the seal, he took only what he needed. Joe had no patience with white men who hunted for sport and killed game they couldn't possibly use.

They were close to the falls now and had to shout to make themselves heard over the sullen roar of the water. From an open space in the forest, they had a good view as the big stream tumbled down a mountain in a series of falls at least a mile long. The last plunge—about a hundred feet—crashed into a big pool on level ground near the beach, and a wide creek poured out of it and quickly flowed into the salt water.

The pool was half hidden behind a fringe of willows, and it seemed to be boiling. Chet and Joe suddenly raced down a deer trail toward it, and Tommy followed them. His short legs had to take two steps to the bigger boys' one, but he was close behind them when they burst through the willows at the water's edge. There in the big pool they saw hundreds of humpback salmon in a frenzy. Tommy thought they must have all gone crazy. Many of them lay on their sides thrashing violently without going anywhere.

Tommy and Chet looked at Joe, and he explained what was happening.

"They are burying their eggs in sand so the trout won't eat them," Joe said.

Maybe they buried some of the eggs, but Tommy saw thousands of them in the water. Dolly Varden trout dashed in to seize some of the eggs, but they turned and darted just as quickly away to avoid the clashing jaws of the larger salmon. There were many other trout too, mostly sea run that were about fourteen inches long and covered with yellow spots. The Dolly Varden trout that had never been in seawater had bright crimson spots.

Salmon had been spawning here for about two weeks. Hundreds of dead ones lay on the bottom in still water near the edge of the pool. Joe scooped up an egg and showed it to Tommy. A tiny fish head stuck out of one side of it and a little tail out of the other. In the red transparent egg, he could see a backbone connecting the head and tail. In crevices between stones, he could see fully formed fish, some of them were barely a half-inch long.

"The dead ones rot," Chet said. "Tiny particles of the meat feed the spawn. In a little while, they will be fingerlings; then they will go out to salt water."

Tommy only half-heard his brother over the roar of falling water, and he really didn't care because he had something else on his mind. Tommy and Joe had brought along fishhooks and short pieces of line. They cut willow wands for poles and fished for the Dolly Varden trout they had seen.

Chet lay under a tree and made sarcastic remarks. Fishing for sluggish Dolly Varden wasn't his idea of sport. "When I fish for trout, I want a fly rod and rainbow or cutthroats that can give me a battle!" he shouted.

Tommy paid no attention to him. He thought that a Dolly tasted as good as any other trout. Besides, he thought any trout would be a nice change from Peg Leg's cooking. There was so much bait in the water, it was just an accident if a trout took an egg with a hook in it, but there were so many fish a person was bound to hook one now and then. They just yanked the fish out, threw them up on the bank and cast for another one. Tommy hurled a big one back over his head, and it slipped off the hook and landed in the sand close to the willows. He left it there and baited his hook again.

Joe shouted something. Tommy didn't catch the words, but Joe was laughing and pointing. Tommy turned in time to see the raccoon slip into the willows with the big trout in its mouth.

Tommy didn't mind. There were plenty of trout, and they had nearly as many as they could eat. He caught another, and then he hurled one up by the willows and slyly watched to see what would happen. Sure enough, a gray face with a burglar mask on it peeked at him out of a clump of ferns. Tommy didn't turn his head to look directly at it, and soon the raccoon ran out and seized the fish. It stood a moment, seemed to grin at him, then turned and walked slowly into the brush with a derisive wave of his bushy tail.

Tommy didn't understand how the furry face could appear to be laughing at him, but he was certain it was. A little later, he saw the old robber come out to the creek to wash the fish before eating it. There were so many trout, he could have caught his own, but this raccoon seemed to think they tasted better if he stole them. After a time, Tommy saw him slip back into the ferns to wait for another donation.

Chet was watching too. "That old raccoon has a rubber stomach like Tommy's!" he shouted. "It can keep eating all day."

The raccoon looked at Chet for a moment, then slipped away. Later, Tommy saw it swim across the mouth of the creek and amble on down the beach.

Awhile after Joe built a fire and cooked the fish on a heated flat rock, Tommy noticed that Chet had eaten more than his share. Maybe a Dolly Varden wasn't a sporty fish, but it tasted great when it was pulled out of cold water and cooked almost before it quit wiggling.

Tommy and Joe saw the raccoon again the next week. It was robbing a grouse nest, crushing the eggs in its mouth, and sucking on them happily before spitting out the shells. The bird sat on a limb above it and scolded in angry little clucking sounds.

"They always steal from somebody," Joe said with a shake of his head.

Tommy felt sorry for the grouse, but just the same, the big raccoon was kind of a loveable old bandit.

Chapter 10

The Devil Fish

Tommy stood in the bow of the big dory, rubbing a file over a jigger to make it shiny. It was made of lead and tin that was molded in the shape of a fish about eight inches long. Two cod hooks were set in the head and a wire leader was attached to a hole in the tail.

Chet sat in the stern, pulling his line up four or five feet in a jerky motion, letting the jigger sink down to the bottom, then jerking it up again. A long cod and two rock cod flopped in a fish box between them.

"This isn't my idea of sport fishing," Chet grumbled, "just hauling them up by brute force."

Tommy preferred fishing for trout with a fly rod too, or for salmon with a trawling rod, but he also enjoyed this bottom fishing. A person never knew what he'd hook into next, maybe a bass or red snapper. If they were very lucky, they might get a black cod or a chicken halibut—one under 50 pounds. Of course, they caught a lot of trashy fish such as dogfish, ratfish, bullhead, or skate. They were annoyances, but it was nice out here in the middle of the lagoon on a sunny August day, enjoying the cool breeze blowing up South Bentinck Arm.

Tommy dropped his jigger over the side, and it went down and down, thirty fathoms—a hundred and eighty feet—before it hit bottom. He jerked it up as far as his arms would reach. The jigger would be coming up tail first. A cod would have to be mighty silly to think any fish swam like that, but maybe cod were as dumb as they looked.

Pinky was rafting logs a half mile off to the left. He waved at them and Chet waved back, but Tommy's jigger had come against something solid, and he was busy hauling in on the line. Whatever it was felt very heavy, probably a lingcod. Suddenly it ran toward the stern of the boat. If it tangled the lines, Chet would be cross, so Tommy pulled it in frantically. Still, he remembered that he must coil the line carefully in a box so it wouldn't tangle when he let it out again. Chet wouldn't like that either. Now the fish was coming straight up, and Tommy had pulled in most of his line. He looked over the side, and in the clear water he could see the fish about a dozen feet down.

Wow! It was an ugly-looking thing. The slender, three-foot-long body was similar in shape to a cultus cod, but it had a huge head with a flat face. Two glassy, pale eyes about the size of half-dollars stared up at him. The eyes stuck out about two inches. Tommy wasn't sure he wanted this horrible-looking creature in any boat he was in, so he stopped pulling in the line. Now the fish drifted to the surface, and it looked even more grotesque. What looked like part of the fish's guts stuck out of its mouth. Tommy knew that this happened when you pulled a fish up fast out of very deep water, but it was disturbing to see. The big fish was gray with black spots, and it had a row of needle-sharp spines along its back. Chet told him to be careful, because he would have a very sore hand if he touched the spines. He jerked on the line, hoping to tear the hook loose so the fish would go away, but the hook was set solid. Chet was grinning at him.

"Cultus cod," he said. "Not what you could call pretty but tastes as good as any of the cod. Gaff it and throw it aboard."

Tommy made a feeble pass at it with the gaff, a big hook lashed to a short pole. He didn't try very hard to hit the ugly thing, but at the same time, he knew that he had to get his jigger out of it somehow.

Chet tied his line around a tholepin and came forward disgustedly. He jerked the gaff into the fish and threw it into the box.

"Are you going to be a baby all your life?" he grumbled. "If you're old enough to fish, you're old enough to gaff them for yourself. Take the hook out of it."

It looked like an entirely different fish now. The spines were hinged and they lay flat on its back. The eyes were pulled in, and they seemed to look at him out of deep sockets. It still looked ugly, and he didn't want to touch it, but Chet was watching him and shaking his head.

Tommy caught the jigger and yanked the hook out of the cod's mouth. He felt a little silly about being afraid of it when it was flopping around harmlessly in the box. Chet didn't have to be so nasty about it. He'd probably been scared too when he saw his first cultus cod. It was easy enough to be brave when you knew about things and what to do about them.

Tommy shined his jigger, and Chet was back in the stern, jerking his bait up and letting it sink back. Then he hooked something and was hauling in on the line. The fish seemed heavy as Chet kept pulling. Tommy wanted to go back and help, but maybe Chet would be mad.

"Halibut," Chet panted. "I've got a real fish!" After a time, the fish seemed to come up a little easier. Chet was able to drag it to the surface. It was a big flat fish, almost square, with a dark gray back, but the belly was snow white. Chet heaved it aboard.

"An eighteen-pounder," he crowed. "That's as big as we get them in here. The bigger ones go out into deep water. Look at its eyes. When these fish are very small, they swim upright like other fish, and there's an eye on each side of the head. Then they get bigger and lay flat on the bottom. The lower eye migrates halfway around the head so both eyes look straight up."

The fish arched itself on its head and tail, and its body came down with a hard thump that threatened to pound the bottom out of the boat. Since no amount of clubbing would kill it, Chet set a hook in its nose and looped a short line around the tail. He pulled the line tight so the halibut could only rock back and forth. That seemed like a cruel thing to do, but it solved the problem. Tommy just wished it wouldn't take so long to die.

The dory had swung around so the stern was toward the narrow channel at the mouth of the lagoon. The tide had turned. Tommy pulled in the anchor line until he lifted the light hook thirty or forty feet off the bottom, and Chet rowed the boat to the other side of a rocky reef. Tommy dropped the anchor when Chet told him to, and then watched as his brother let the tide drift the boat until a dry snag on shore was in line with the corner of the cookhouse. That, Chet said, would put them directly over the reef. He took two half turns around the bow post to hold the dory in position.

They had all the fish the loggers could eat, but they might get better ones. Anyway, Joe's people could always use any that Peg Leg didn't want. The boys were excited and wanted to keep on fishing.

Chet hooked a ratfish and yanked the hook out of it with disgust. It had a shark's head and tail but was small—the smallest of the shark family. When Chet threw it back into the water, it drifted away on the current. After a while, it would adjust to the lighter pressure at the surface and gradually work down into deep water again.

Tommy's hook slammed into something solid and so heavy he could hardly lift it. Whatever it was didn't wiggle, and it came up like a sack of sand. He braced his feet against the dory side and dragged line in over the gunnel a foot at a time. "Help me, Chet. I can't lift it," he pleaded. But Chet had hooked a big cultus cod and didn't have time to bother with his little brother.

Tommy brought his catch up about fifty feet. He tried but he couldn't hold on any longer, and it dropped back to the bottom. The fast-moving line burned his hands, so he put on cotton gloves and tried again. Still, the thing wouldn't budge. Chet landed his cod and came forward. He took the line from Tommy and heaved up as hard as he could.

"You're hooked to a rock," he said impatiently. "We'll just have to cut the line."

"It's alive," Tommy insisted. "I had it up quite a way, but it swam back to the bottom, and I couldn't hold it."

Chet tried again and Tommy pulled with him. "It could be one of those three- or four-hundred-pound halibut they catch sometimes out in deep water," Chet mused, "but I wouldn't expect to hook one in here."

They both braced their feet against the side of the boat and heaved with every ounce of strength in them. It wouldn't budge. Chet took out his pocketknife and opened it.

"If you did have a fish on it, the thing's tangled you around a rock by now. I'll just have to cut the line."

"No," Tommy protested. "It's Pinky's line. If we lose thirty fathoms of it, there won't be enough left to be any good to him."

Chet raked his fingers through his curly red hair. He always did that when he was working out a problem. Tommy waited quietly. Chet was fourteen and resourceful. He would find a way to solve their problem.

"We don't want to cut the line, and we can't sit here holding on to it forever," Chet said. "So, I'll pull up on it as hard as I can, and when there is slack you can take a turn of it around the thwart. The line isn't strong enough to tip over this big dory, so the rising tide will break it. Maybe the leader will break or the line will part far enough down so we won't lose too much of it."

Chet managed to pull in several feet of line, and Tommy tightened it around the thwart as he had been instructed. Then they sat and looked at it for a long time. The dory canted over gradually. When the gunnel was only two feet out of water, Tommy thought there must be at least five hundred pounds of strain on the line. Chet laid the open knife on the thwart where he could reach it quickly, just in case.

The dory righted itself with a rush, and the line went slack. Chet started pulling it in to see how much of it was left, and Tommy untied it from the thwart. He had pulled in thirty or forty feet of line when he felt the heavy weight again.

Together they heaved in line slowly and felt a hard jerk on it from time to time. Sweat poured out of their hair and down their faces. Tommy passed a bight of the line around the thwart so they could stop and rest a moment. Then they took in the slack as fast as Chet could pull it in.

"Whatever it is, it seems to be alive," Chet gasped. "But no halibut was ever as heavy as this. Darned if I know what we have on this line."

They pulled in twenty fathoms of line, then twenty-five. Tommy peeked over the side. There was something big and dark down there, but he couldn't make out what it was. Chet had pulled in another six or eight feet when the line suddenly went slack. Tommy felt a little sick. They had torn loose from the thing just when they were getting it close enough to have a look at it.

Then something bumped hard against the bottom of the boat. Long, snaky arms reached high out of the water on both sides of it. Tommy screamed and Chet yelled, "Octopus! Get down flat in the bottom of the boat, Tommy."

Tommy was crouching in the boat with his face pressed into the narrow V at the bow, the boat's ribs pushing hard against his temples. He thought his buttocks were too high, and he tried to slide back so he could lie flat on the bottom, but something was holding him back. One of the long arms was wrapped around his lower leg, and it held on fiercely. The boat was filled with frenzied screams. Tommy didn't know if he made them or Chet did, or if they came from the octopus. Maybe it had already dragged Chet overboard, but the screams went on and on.

Then Chet's voice cut through the screams and confusion. "Lie still, Tommy. Don't struggle. It can't hurt us. After a while it will go away."

Tommy twisted his face around, but he couldn't see Chet. He saw a snaky tentacle curl around the oars and pull them over the side. One of them was wrapped around his leg and a board in the false bottom of the boat. Maybe if it weren't for that board, he would have been pulled over too. Tentacles were wrapped around thwarts and tholepins. He noticed tentacles were on both sides of the boat, so the octopus couldn't tip it over. One of them swept over close above him and settled across the fish box. The slender tip wrapped around a thwart, and Tommy could see little suction cups the whole length of it.

Chet's voice came to Tommy again. "Lie still, Tommy. I'm coming." He saw Chet's face under the thwart.

Chet looked scared too. He was wedged between the fish box and the side of the dory and pulling himself under the thwart. Tommy watched him through a film of tears. The tentacles were no longer waving around in the air. Now, they had fastened themselves to the boat and one was still around Tommy's leg. Chet's hand was on his ankle, but the leg was numb, and Tommy could hardly feel it. Chet was slashing at the tentacle around his leg and Tommy was screaming again.

"No, Chet, no! You'll just make him madder!"

Chet kept on slashing. He always kept his knife razor sharp, but the octopus tentacle seemed as tough as manila rope. And then the pressure was gone from Tommy's leg. Chet pulled him back so he was lying flat in the boat. Tommy tried to make himself as small as possible.

The tentacle was waving in the air again, and there was a jagged tip where Chet had cut it loose from Tommy's leg. As Chet was sliding back under the thwart, the tentacle seemed to be reaching for him or for Chet. Tommy tried to hide his face, but he couldn't. His eyes kept following the horrible thing until it wrapped itself around the bow post. Then he became aware of the sound of a motor very close to them.

Chet was looking over the gunnel and yelling, "Don't come any closer, Joe. He'll upset your canoe."

Tommy lifted his head to look over the side. Joe was circling around the stern in a canoe with an outboard motor. Two of the tentacles seemed to stretch out toward the canoe but couldn't reach it. Soon, Joe was around beside the dory. Then he cut in sharply across the bow and reached down into the water with his fish gaff. The tide was running hard, so the anchor line was stretched out tight, and Joe caught it.

The two tentacles were waving over the dory again, so Tommy flopped back down on the floor. As the sound of the motor was getting farther away, he heard a new noise: oarlocks. He heard Pinky's voice say, "Sit tight, Chet. I'll get him."

The tentacles had caught their dory again, and Tommy peeked enough to look over the gunnel. Pinky was coming toward them, standing up in a skiff, facing the bow and rowing fast. Joe had the boys' anchor in the canoe and was towing the dory toward the point. Pinky bent down so he could look under the dory, and then he headed toward its stern at an angle that would bring him close. He took in his oars, picked up a pike pole, and stood waiting in the skiff. The tentacles on one side let go of the dory and reached for the skiff. That made the other side of the dory cant down until it seemed as if it would tip over. The tentacles were now holding on to the skiff and one of them was wrapped around Pinky's waist. The dory and the skiff were coming together fast, and when they were close enough, Pinky began thrusting the steel-tipped pike pole under the dory. He stabbed again and again with it. Then the boats bumped together, and Pinky stepped over into the dory.

The tentacles had let go and the jigger line was running out slowly. Pinky grabbed it and began pulling in on it. A voice was screaming, "No, Pinky, let it go away!" Tommy realized that it was his own voice as he looked up at a smiling Pinky.

"I thought you were a real fisherman, Tommy. You wouldn't let a big one like this get away, would you? Give me a hand, both of you. He's dead."

Chet stood up and began pulling on the line, but he looked a little shaky. After a while, Tommy stood up too. When he gazed down into the clear water, he could see a big, olive-green ball that was the octopus. Its tentacles hung straight down, and they weren't moving.

Joe, watching from the canoe, had towed them out of the strong current and was sweeping them toward the shore. The canoe was very close to the beach and Black Bill, the blacksmith, was wading into the water to pull the octopus to the shore. Spike was hurrying down the beach toward them. Tommy grabbed the jigger line and tried to do his part, but his legs were kind of wobbly, and he had to hold on to the boat with one hand.

The six of them dragged the dead octopus onto the beach. Out of the water, it looked as big as a bear. The tentacles were about ten feet long; close to the body, they were as big around as Tommy's waist, and they tapered down to the size of his wrist near the tip. It had a hooked beak like an eagle, but it was much larger. It hung from a ragged flap of white flesh that was almost transparent. The eight-inch tip of Pinky's pike pole had torn a big hole above the beak. With one slash of the big pocketknife Pinky always carried, he severed it completely and handed the beak to Tommy for a souvenir.

"Lots of food!" Joe said excitedly.

Tommy felt a little sick. "You wouldn't eat that awful-looking thing, would you?" he asked.

Joe smiled. "The devil fish is good the way my people cook it."

"Better give it all to them," Spike muttered. "Peg Leg won't cook it, and I won't eat it."

"I will," Pinky said. "I want a big feed off it when you get it cooked, Joe."

The octopus must have weighed more than half a ton, so they had to chop it into chunks to pack it in Joe's canoe. The meat didn't look so bad when it was skinned. Tommy thought he might be able to eat it if he didn't know it was octopus.

Pinky pointed out the brain, close to the surface right behind the beak and near the small black eyes. "It's easy to kill them if you know where to strike," he told Chet as they went out in the dory to get the skiff and gather up oars, gaffs, pike pole, and equipment that seemed to be scattered all over the lagoon. Tommy decided not to stay with them. He only wanted to go up to his room and stretch out on the bed. He didn't even want supper.

A few days later, Tommy and Chet were out on the boom with Pinky when Joe brought over a pail full of cooked octopus meat. It had the texture of crab meat. Tommy bravely nibbled a little piece of it and decided that it *tasted* something like crab meat. He ate his share of it and maybe a little more.

Chapter 11

Amateur Archeology

Tommy, Chet, and Talyu Joe walked directly into a rainbow. It was the brightest and prettiest rainbow Tommy had ever seen, and he'd never been so close to one. The boys were walking down an old trail toward Owikeno Lake in the hot August sunshine, a small creek gurgling and splashing beside them. The ground beneath their feet was getting muddy. A shiny gray curtain seemed to hang across the trail in front of them and in it were two rainbows. A large one reached completely across the valley and rested on the mountains on either side, and a small rainbow inside the big one barely spanned the trail ahead. It looked like a round-topped door and Joe, who was leading, walked through it.

Chet followed Joe and just disappeared. Tommy stepped through, out of bright sunlight and into what felt like a waterfall. Cold rain beat through his thin shirt, making him shiver. This was the first rain they had seen in nearly three months so, of course, they weren't dressed for it.

Chet backed into Tommy and pushed him out into the bright sunlight again. They could almost reach out and touch the rainbow's violet band. Tommy wanted to go through it again and find Joe, maybe in a fairyland at the other side of the rainbow. But Chet was grumbling, "Our last camping trip of the summer and we have to run into something like this."

Joe came back to them. As usual, he wore only overalls and moccasins. In the sunlight, his shirtless wet skin looked dark bronze. His long black hair was plastered to his head, but his dark eyes were dancing.

"A little rain won't hurt us," he grinned, "but it gets food and blankets wet. Let's wait until the rain goes away." He dropped the long-handled shovel he was carrying and set his knapsack on a rock. It contained the food Peg Leg had put up for them.

Chet put a roll of blankets wrapped in canvas on the rock and leaned a mattock against it. His red hair was getting long too. It was generally curly, but now it was wet and plastered down. His light green shirt stuck to his narrow shoulders and back.

Tommy put down the two jointed fly rods and reel he was carrying near the rock with their other gear. The blue shirt he wore was stuck to his skin too, but it felt kind of good in the warm sunshine. They stood and watched the gray curtain and the rainbows move slowly away from them and down the valley.

"The rain won't last long," Joe said. "Come on. I'll show you where the weather gods make wind and rain."

Chet muttered something about Nuxalk superstitions, but he followed Joe and Tommy as they angled up the steep slopes to a round-topped knoll. Tommy heard something that sounded like the rustle of many wings, but there were no birds in sight.

Joe pointed to a narrow notch between two snow-capped peaks a long way above them. A fluffy white cloud swirled out of it and scudded down the valley toward Owikeno Lake.

"Weather gods live in a little valley up there," Joe told them. "They make the wind; it blows up there all summer long."

"That pass must extend all the way through the range," Chet responded. "Warm air from the interior rises and blows through it, and at that altitude it gets chilled. Down here there is warm, moist air from Queen Charlotte Sound. That mix causes the rain."

But Joe wasn't finished, and he continued with his story. "Long time ago, in the days of my grandfathers, two of our men climbed up there to see the weather gods at work. They never came back. Gods don't like people to spy on them."

"Nuts!" Chet exclaimed. "They probably fell off a cliff, or the Wuikinuxv people got them."

"Maybe," Joe said, "but my people don't go up there to look for them." He turned and led the way back to their packs, and Tommy was afraid his feelings had been hurt. Of course, Chet was probably right. He was in high school and knew about things like that, but why did he always have to show off and let people know how smart he was? Tommy liked Joe's idea better.

The gray curtain had moved a mile down the valley. They followed it slowly in ankle-deep mud. The creek was much bigger now. It roared and splashed, and rocks rolling along the bottom made hollow booming sounds. Steam rose from the wet ground. The air was hot and sultry.

When they caught up with the rainbow again, Chet sat down on a rock to wait for it to move on. Tommy stripped off his sweaty clothes and stepped into the rain just because it felt so good when he was out in the warm sun again. Joe took off his moccasins and overalls too and dashed into the rain, daring Tommy to follow him. His voice sounded muffled and far off. Tommy plunged into the rain. After a moment, the cold was gone and he felt good. Something big loomed up ahead of him. It looked like a brown bear. When Tommy crashed into it, big arms were around him. He screamed, but he knew it was Joe the whole time. They wrestled and rolled around in the yellow clay. Tommy managed to sit on Joe's stomach and pin his shoulders to the ground, but of course, it was only because Joe let him. Even Chet couldn't pin Joe, and they both knew it.

They were plastered with mud when they got up laughing and calling for Chet to join them. Rain made little rivers down their backs washing off the mud.

Chet stayed where he was. After a time, the curtain turned silvery. The sun looked like a pale white moon. It turned to gold, and they were in the sunshine again. The rain had washed them clean, and they stood at a mossy spot to let the sun dry them before putting on their clothes.

Chet was grumbling. "At this rate, we won't get to the lake in time to do any digging today. How far is it?"

"It's not far," Joe answered. "Mile … maybe mile and a half. We have plenty of time."

As they started to walk again, Tommy asked apprehensively, "Won't the Wuikinuxv people be mad if they see us digging in the mounds?"

Joe shook his head. "They won't care. We don't fight the Wuikinuxv people anymore."

They followed the rain as it moved slowly down the valley, pausing only to eat sour red huckleberries and blueberries from high bushy plants. The sun slid behind a mountain and the rainbows were gone. A dozen geese circled high above a small lake. Over the center of it, each bird folded one wing and fell several yards straight down before opening the wing to check the fall and folding the other one. They came down in a series of short plunges and leveled off close to the water. There was almost no splash when they landed.

"Smart birds," Chet said. "A hunter hidden in the bushes wouldn't have been in shotgun range of them."

"Those geese have been shot at," Joe explained, "so they won't circle low over bushes anymore."

The creek was becoming a river, getting wider and more sluggish. Joe turned to the left and led them around the shoulder of a mountain, and soon they were headed down into another valley. Now they walked under big Douglas firs, dry needles crackling under their feet. A dozen yards away, willows along a lakeshore were half hidden in the curtain of rain. Another river, a much bigger one, poured into the lake. It was crystal clear but sluggish too. Despite the rain along the river, there had certainly been none in this valley. As they stood there by the river, deciding what to do next, a very large salmon silently swam by them.

"Wuikinuxv people get big salmon," Joe said wistfully. "Six-year run. Fifty-, sixty-, maybe even eighty-pound fish. At the Talyu River, we had four-year runs, salmon weighing twenty, thirty, or sometimes forty pounds."

They were on a little peninsula between the two rivers, and Chet began running toward four low mounds arranged in a square. Each mound was about twenty feet wide, eighty feet long, and about two feet high. Chet began tearing sod and bushes with the mattock from the corner of one of them. Tommy and Joe hurried over to watch. Chet was swinging the mattock like a crazy person. They could see that Chet had pulled away the sod and under the sod were about four inches of black loam, and under that a thinner layer of gray ash and charred wood.

When the mattock made a crunching sound, Chet threw it aside and began to paw at the ground with his hands. He quickly pulled out several pieces of porcelain that appeared to have been a bowl. If it wasn't damaged already, the mattock had broken it into small pieces. Chet wrapped them in a piece of paper from the knapsack.

"Just in case we don't find bigger pieces," he said, "the school museum can glue these together."

It seemed silly to Tommy. What would anyone want with old broken dishes? Joe was cutting out squares of sod with the small shovel they had brought along. "Maybe we'll find an arrowhead or a stone axe," he said, so Tommy found a sharp stick and started digging too.

Joe found a few very small pieces of a bowl. Chet said they weren't big enough, and there weren't enough of them to be worth saving. He was digging more carefully, and he found another layer of ash about six inches below the first one.

"The village burned down twice," Joe told them, "maybe more than twice." Below another five inches of the loam, he found more ash, then another eight inches of loam, and yet another layer of ash on yellow clay. Four big lodges had burned down here. In the lower layer of ash, Chet found a black arrowhead, but it was so crumbly he couldn't save it.

"They made arrowheads out of obsidian at the time of that fire," Chet explained. "It doesn't stand heat as a flint would."

Joe found a bone fishhook and a flint awl in the loam under the top layer of ash. Tommy dug a yellow arrowhead and a black one out of the loam under the third layer. Chet was excited about his brother's find. This was something he had read about, and he was eager to share his knowledge.

"They were using both obsidian and flint when that lodge burned, maybe six or eight hundred years ago," Chet said.

"The Wuikinuxv people must have had some contact with other First Nations people from the interior and learned how to use both. Knight Inlet runs all the way through these mountains. Talyu people came here to trade with Kwalhna people," Joe added, expanding on Chet's history lesson.

Dusk settled in under the trees, but the gray curtain had moved, and Tommy could see three or four miles down the lake. Mountains to the east were still in bright sunlight and stood out sharply against a pale blue sky.

"It's time to make camp, Tommy," Joe said. "Let Chet dig. You can cut the boughs for the roof and for a deep springy bed." Joe knew exactly how to proceed, and, in a very short time, they had a snug camp with a fire burning before it. Soon Joe was frying bacon and potatoes for their supper.

When Chet rushed into camp excitedly with a piece of red pottery, Tommy and Joe examined the find with very little interest. It was about as big as Tommy's hand and appeared to be part of a big red bowl. There were crisscross markings on the outside.

Joe handed it back to Chet. "Supper is ready," was all he said.

But Chet persisted. "Don't you know what this is?" he asked. "It's important. It's one of the first cooking pots, a clay-lined basket. They used to boil meat in them by dropping hot stones into the water. I found it in the lower layer of ash. It must be a thousand years old! I'll try to figure out its age more precisely tomorrow."

"A good trick if you can do it," Tommy said doubtfully. "How are you going to do that?"

"Well," Chet began, "that last fire must have been about a hundred years ago. There are six inches between it and the second layer, so the second fire must have occurred about 250 years ago."

Joe dished up their meal, and Chet wiped his hands on his pants without bothering to wash. Tommy was sure that their dad wouldn't be happy if he knew about it, but then again, this was a camping trip. Maybe Dad wouldn't mind.

Chet looked disappointed. He scratched a greasy finger through his hair. But he could always come up with an answer. "Next summer, I'll roll a log over the upper layer of loam until it is packed, then measure it," he said triumphantly. "Maybe we can find the stubs of totem poles or log uprights. Their rings will fit the time. Cedar won't rot much in a thousand years in this wet clay. At the university, they have a tree-ring pattern that goes back a long time. Some years the tree grows fast, and the space between rings is wide. In dry years or years with a short growing season, the space is narrow. We have looked at rings that cover a very long time, and we never find the same sequence of rings."

Tommy stretched out on the bed he had made from boughs, and soon Chet's voice became just a drone. Then Joe was talking excitedly.

"In the days of my grandfather's grandfather, warriors followed the trail one night. They knew where the Wuikinuxv sentinel who watched the trail would be. They sneaked up on him, killed him, and then shot fire arrows into the Illahee people. The Wuikinuxv people got away, and they took many young girls with them; one of them was my grandfather's mother."

As Tommy stared into the fire, it became a great conflagration. And he was in the middle of it. Four big lodges were burning. Men were rushing out of them. They wore feathers on their mostly bare skin and paint in patterns of reds, blacks, and whites. The men stopped to look at him, eyes wide, and suddenly they shouted in words Tommy couldn't understand.

Tommy woke up screaming. Chet was gently holding his shoulder. "Wake up, little brother," he said, smiling. "You've been having another nightmare."

"I scared you with talk about fighting, Tommy," Joe said. "Don't worry. That was a long time ago. We don't fight now. The last big battle happened when my grandfather was young. That battle was on an island white people call Slaughter Illahee at the mouth of River's Inlet. My people and 'Namgis warriors fought the Wuikinuxv people. Nearly all the Wuikinuxv people were killed, so there aren't many left."

Chet probably didn't even hear Joe. He was busy sorting his treasures and making plans for tomorrow. Tommy soon was back to sleep. When he woke up, it was daylight. He realized he was alone in the lean-to, and he was a little frightened, but then he saw Chet digging at the mound and Joe fishing in the clear water river. Tommy scrambled into his clothes and grabbed a fly rod.

Joe had already caught all the fish they could eat, but Tommy caught two more ten-inch rainbows just to be sure there would be enough. Joe pointed to a bald eagle perched on a limb of a dead snag across the river. "Watch him," he said. "Little birds will drive him crazy."

Several small black birds darted close to the eagle, but veered away before the massive bird could strike them. The little birds were smaller than the head of the eagle, but as the eagle turned toward a bird bothering it on one side, another small bird darted in to strike at the back of his head. They couldn't have been hurting the eagle very much, but its thin scream sounded angry when it spread its wings and began an upward spiral, up and up until Tommy thought it must be higher than the mountains. Up there, it looked as small as the little birds that had driven it from its perch.

"Little birds can't fly so high," Joe explained. "Black birds hate the eagle and raven; they always pick on them. Come on, let's find Chet."

They found him at the mounds, and Joe joined Chet in the quest for more artifacts. The older boys dug all morning, but Tommy lost interest after scratching at the dig with a sharp stick, the best digging tool he could find. Tommy went down to the lakeshore and thought again how beautiful it was with upside-down mountains in all its forty-mile length. Mountain goats played on a cliff just a few yards above the lake, and their pictures were upside down in the water too. A big yellow cinnamon bear came out of the brush across the river and stood looking at him. Tommy decided it was time to return to the mound.

"He won't eat you," Joe grinned. "He likes salmon better. Come on, we'll get some lunch."

Joe made coffee, and they ate the sandwiches and cake Peg Leg had put up for them. Dad wouldn't let Tommy drink coffee at the camp unless it was half milk, but he drank it now along with his two companions. He especially enjoyed it because this was a camping trip and coffee brewed in a tin can over a campfire always tasted better than it did at home.

Chet and Joe bolted their lunch and hurried back to the mound, but Tommy was eating a big piece of devil's food cake and took time to enjoy it. When he returned to the mound, he saw that Joe was digging a big obsidian axe out of the loam under the top layer of ash. The blade was buried deep in the dirt, so the fire hadn't damaged it. There had been a sharp point at the back of it like the pick on a prospector's hammer. Now it was broken into two small pieces, but Chet said he could glue it together, and Joe gave him the axe for the school museum.

Tommy found a steel knife and handed it to Chet. "This knife proves the Wuikinuxv people had dealings with white men a hundred years ago," Chet said. There was no temper left in the blade, but Chet was glad to get it.

Soon, Chet's mattock scraped on something, and he began pawing at the ground with his hands. He dug out something round and mottled brown in color, picked it up, and then dropped it as if it had burned his fingers. It rolled over, and they were confronted with black teeth grinning up at them. Tommy yelled and backed away from it, but Joe picked up the skull and examined it critically. He removed a flint arrowhead from an eye socket. It was square at the top and had sharp corners.

"One of our people," he said. "Wuikinuxv people's arrowheads are round at the top." Joe offered it to Tommy, but he pulled his hands away and stepped back.

"I don't want it. I'm leaving this place."

After he returned to camp, Tommy felt a little silly about being afraid of the ugly thing, but just the same, a skull was the scariest part of a skeleton.

While Tommy waited in their camp, the older boys searched for a time, resolved to find more bones. Then they joined Tommy who was glad they were all together again.

"It's one o'clock. If we are going to get home in time for supper, we'd better get started," Chet said regretfully, as he packed his treasures in his blanket roll. Joe put the skull in his knapsack. Tommy thought it was a gruesome thing to save as a souvenir.

"I'm going to spend a lot of time up here next summer," Chet said as they headed back up the trail. "Maybe we can find a whole skeleton."

Tommy sniffed. Let Chet and Joe search for old bones. He'd go fishing.

Chapter 12

Tenas Mowitch

It was nice out on the water in the late evening with just enough of a breeze blowing up South Bentinck Arm to drive away the mosquitoes. It blew through Tommy's thin shirt, and he felt comfortably cool after the heat of the day. The breeze ruffled Chet's curly red hair. The ripples it caused on the water made little whispering sounds along the beach.

Days were getting shorter in mid-August, but at eight o'clock, sunlight still caused a pink glow on the snowfield at the top of The Mountain beside them. Now deep dusk was moving into the forest along the shore, and there was a tingling, shivery feel in it. Almost anything could be happening back there under the trees. Band-tailed pigeons cooed softly, and the staccato whistle of a raccoon came from down the beach. Up in the mountains, a great horned owl was hooting.

Across the big lagoon, lights from the logging camp were getting brighter, each one making a little golden path on the water. In another two weeks, vacation would be over, and Tommy and his older brother would have to return to Hastings Academy in Vancouver. Tommy tried to keep from thinking about it as he sprawled in the stern of the skiff while Chet rowed lazily along the shoreline. Sure, Dad said they could come up here again next summer, but that seemed an awfully long time to wait.

Fish darted away from the boat in every direction, making streaks of white, phosphorescent flame. Drops of the fire hung from Chet's oars each time he lifted them from the water. Off to the left, a big creek tumbled down The Mountain in a series of white falls. The last one plunged a hundred feet into a big pool on a gravelly point that was formed by debris washed down from The Mountain. A big stream flowed out of it on the south side. Sometimes Tommy, Chet, and Joe fished in it for trout. A game trail angled up the slope from the pool. They had climbed up it once and followed the trail far up The Mountain. But right now, the boys heard the high-pitched sounds of coyotes barking and yelping excitedly. Tommy quickly sat up and looked questioningly at his brother.

"They're chasing a deer," Chet whispered, "and they'll kill it if they can catch it. But maybe they won't. They're coming down the trail, and if the deer can get to the beach, it will be safe. Coyotes won't follow it into the water."

Chet rested on his oars a hundred yards offshore. The clamor came closer. It seemed funny that coyotes and wolves made such a racket when they were hunting. If they sneaked up on their prey silently as a cougar did, they would have an easier time catching it. But then again, it was fortunate they didn't. A deer wouldn't have a chance against them unless it had a head start.

The noisy animals were getting very close. Tommy held his breath. Of all the wild creatures, he loved deer the best. They were such beautiful, graceful things, and around the logging camp they were quite tame. Sometimes he could get very close to them before they bounded away.

A shadowy something darted out of the fringe of the scrub willows by the pool. It was indistinct in the deepening darkness, but it was certainly a deer. Nothing else bounced along like that. Tommy let out his breath explosively as the deer plunged into the water. A smaller animal followed close behind, and without hesitation it bounded into the water too.

"This is a new one on me," Chet gasped. "I have never heard of a coyote following a deer into the water."

"It will catch the deer. Help him, Chet," Tommy pleaded.

The deer swam toward them as if it were coming for help, and Chet rowed to meet it. Several light gray shadows showed for a moment at the edge of the willows, then quickly went back into them. The deer was quite close, and Tommy could see big mule ears. It was a doe. The tip of Chet's oar nearly brushed against it as he passed the deer and swung the boat between the deer and the small animal that pursued it. The little animal seemed to be falling farther behind, but it was close enough for Tommy to catch a glimpse of big ears on it too.

"It's a fawn," he shouted. "A poor tired little fawn. Can't we take him in the boat, Chet? He'll drown."

"A deer, even a fawn, can easily swim across the lagoon," Chet told him. "But he's had a long run, and he does look tired. Maybe we better give him a ride."

The fawn tried to dodge the skiff when Chet backed toward it, but Tommy was able to grasp one of its big ears. He dipped his other arm into the cold water under the fawn and lifted it aboard. He could feel its heart beating hard.

"Don't be afraid, little fellow," he said softly. "I won't hurt you."

It turned its head and pressed a wet nose against Tommy's cheek, making little sniffing sounds. The fawn seemed satisfied that it had found a friend and settled down wearily on Tommy's lap. The doe swam around in circles bleating plaintively.

"She doesn't know what became of her fawn," Chet said. "Lift it up so she can see it, Tommy."

Tommy turned, and the doe saw her fawn. She bleated softly, swam toward the boat, and followed along close behind it as Chet rowed slowly toward camp. She swam as a deer runs, with almost no effort. The doe looked a little scary because her body and legs were covered with what looked like ghostly white fire. Of course, there was no heat in it; everything in the water seemed to be on fire at night. Chet said it came from phosphorous that was produced from rotting vegetation. Tommy wasn't worried about the doe being too tired to keep swimming, even though she had been in the water for a long time. Joe, who seemed to know more than anybody about the woods and mountains and the creatures that lived in them, told him that deer could swim all night if they needed to.

After a few minutes, the doe no longer seemed worried. She swam up so close Tommy could almost touch her. She talked to the fawn, and it answered her in sleepy little bleats. It lay with its head in the crook of Tommy's arm, and he pressed his face against its warm little body.

"They smell friendliness in us like some animals can smell fear or hostility," Chet said. "They run away from the loggers, but we can get very close to them in the woods. Joe can almost pet them."

Tommy pressed his face against the fawn. "I'd like to keep you," he murmured. "I'll call you Tenas Mowitch."

"Tenas Mowitch," Chet repeated. "Chinook for 'little deer.' It's a good name for a fawn, but I'm afraid you'll have to give it back to its mother. She's teaching it how to find other food, but she's still nursing it."

Their father came down to the beach to meet his boys as they grounded the skiff. Tommy scrambled ashore with Tenas Mowitch in his arms, and his father saw what he was carrying. The doe stood in shallow water a short distance away and watched.

"A fawn," he snorted disgustedly. "I can't think of anything we need less around camp. Let it go, Tommy."

Tommy dropped to his knees in the sand and set the fawn on its feet, but he kept an arm around it. There were hot tears close behind his eyes and, even though he tried, he couldn't keep his eyes dry. When Dad spoke in that tone of voice, people seldom argued with him, but Tenas Mowitch was such a loveable little fellow. The fawn pressed hard against him for protection from this new and bigger human.

"If he goes back up on The Mountain, the coyotes will get him," Tommy wailed. "Can't we keep him, Dad?"

"I'm sorry, Tommy," his father said in a gentler tone. "Deer get to be an awful nuisance around camp. Anyway, that fawn needs its mother. You wouldn't take a baby from its mother, would you?"

Pinky, who had been listening to the conversation, joined them. "The game warden wouldn't let you keep it, Tommy," he said, "and a buck gets dangerous if you make a pet of him. One of them mighty near killed the cook when we were working in Moses Inlet. It would have if I hadn't come along with an axe just in time. They can cut a person to ribbons with those sharp hooves."

The doe came out of the water a dozen yards down the beach and bleated plaintively. The fawn trotted toward her, then stopped to look back. It seemed to be begging Tommy to come with them. He watched through a film of tears as doe and fawn faded into the darkness among the bushes behind the blacksmith shop. His father's arm was around Tommy.

"It's better off with its mother," he said again. "In the morning you'll be glad you didn't take it away from her. You'll know it would not be the right thing to do."

Then Chet, who had remained uncharacteristically quiet, added, "Anyway, we'll be going back to Vancouver in two weeks, and we couldn't take a fawn down there; the dogs would get it."

Tommy wiped his tears with a wet sleeve. Dad and Chet were right, of course. Pinky too. But Tenas Mowitch liked him, he was certain, and he was such a special little fawn.

Over the next few days, Tommy and Chet saw many deer in their rambles over the mountains and along the beach. Most of the does had two fawns, but sometimes Tommy saw a mother deer with only one, and he kept wondering if it was Tenas Mowitch. But all the fawns looked alike and not one of them would come to him when he called to it.

There was only one week of vacation left, and the boys wanted to climb all the way to the top of The Mountain. Tommy followed Joe and Chet up a steep game trail. Joe told them he knew of an old rockslide they could climb to the snow line, and it was an easy grade from there to the highest point on the round hump that formed the top of The Mountain.

Halfway to the top, they sat down to rest on a level bench in the rock. There was no wind. The big lagoon and the long inlet looked like green glass far below them. A series of waterfalls on a mountain across from them looked like white lace. The camp and the scar left by logging operations were hidden behind the shoulder of The Mountain. Without that gash in the landscape, it looked really pretty. Tommy searched for a better word, but it was the best he could come up with. Everything was just very pretty. Three miles down South Bentinck Arm, Talyu village seemed to be made of little dollhouses. It seemed to belong in the picture. The scene must have been just like this a hundred years ago before the first white man came to this part of the coast.

Joe seemed to read his thoughts. "It looks even more beautiful from up on top," he said. "From there we can see all the way to Mesachie Head and Dean Channel. Come on. We have a long way to go."

They walked along the bench and it became wider. A cliff formed to the right and water trickled down it in several places, making glistening streaks on the blue granite. Where there were damp spots on the bench, Joe pointed out tracks of deer, bear, and the smaller forest creatures. His sharp eyes never missed anything. Joe caught Tommy's arm and pointed.

"Mowitch," he whispered and drew Tommy down in a clump of high ferns. Chet caught up with them, saw what was happening, and crouched down also.

The deer's tawny color blended into the brown of tree trunks and gray needles, so it took two or three minutes before Tommy spotted it. Then it stood out plain and sharp. It was the big buck he'd seen up by the abandoned logging trestle. There couldn't be two deer with antlers like that in the neighborhood. Chet had thought he'd made up the story about the big buck; now he would have to admit it was true. The antlers were perfectly matched, five points on each side, evenly spaced, and with a beautiful curve to them. On most bucks, the antlers were white or ivory yellow on the points, but these were dark brown right to the tips. It was surely the prettiest deer anyone ever saw.

A small tree had fallen across the trail, shoulder high to the buck, and although he could have ducked his head and walked under it, he stood a moment with his head high, looking over it. Then the forelegs lifted, and he leaped over it with no apparent effort. He just seemed to float over the windfall, landing lightly on the trail.

The deer began to move toward them slowly as if he weren't going anywhere in particular. He walked as if he were out on a morning stroll. After passing half a dozen feet from them, he must have caught their scent. The buck swung his head around and looked directly at them out of startled brown eyes. Then he exploded into action, moving down the trail, bouncing and coming down stiff-legged with all four feet bunched. Then another bounce. His feet seemed to barely brush the ground. With his tail flying like a flag, the big buck was a tawny rubber ball bouncing along. As he faded into the trees, the last thing Tommy saw of the buck was the white of his tail.

"I saw him last summer when he had only four points," Joe said. "I hope no hunter gets him this fall. I want to see him next year, although probably the antlers won't be so pretty by then."

"Do they grow a new point every year?" Tommy asked.

Chet responded in his usual know-it-all way, causing Tommy to feel as though he had asked a dumb question. But at the same time, Tommy realized that Chet probably knew what he was talking about.

"He'll shed his antlers next winter. In the spring he will grow a new set. Tenas Mowitch will have just a straight spike next year. The next one will be a prong horn, then a three pointer. After that he might have three points on one side and four or five on the other. You don't often see anything bigger than a three-pointer evenly matched. This is the first perfect five-pointer I ever saw."

Joe nodded. "Sometimes there's an even number of points, but the points themselves are uneven, long on one side, little nubbins on the other." Joe rose to his feet and started up the trail. Tommy and Chet followed.

At a muddy spot, Joe stopped to examine timber wolf tracks. They were very widely spaced and as big as Tommy's palm.

"A big wolf running very fast," Joe said. "He was chasing a doe and fawn this morning just before the sun came up."

Tommy wondered how he could fix the time so accurately, but he trusted Joe's information, just as he believed what his brother told him about the plants and animals that lived around them. The difference was that most of Chet's information came from books and teachers; most of what Joe told him came from experience and from the traditions of his people.

The three moved on silently until Joe showed them marten tracks and some others he thought had been made by a bushy-tailed rat. The marten had followed the rat into a hole in a pile of rocks. It probably killed the rat and ate it.

A little waterfall tumbled down from the cliff into a pool at the foot of it, and the stream flowed across the bench in a rocky channel. There were bones beside it and tufts of deer hair. The brown stains on the rocks were probably dried blood. Tommy hurried past it. He felt a little sick.

Joe and Chet caught up with him. "Wolf caught the doe," Joe said. "The fawn went this way."

Tommy knew Joe cared about the deer but didn't hate the wolf. Killing was their nature because they had to eat too. Joe liked all the wild creatures, but Tommy hated wolves and coyotes. He didn't want to hear any more talk about the killing, and Joe understood. They walked some distance in silence.

A big fir had fallen across the bench, and the three of them climbed up on it and looked about. Suddenly, a spotted fawn jumped out of a hollow under the root and bounded away a few feet. Then it stopped to look at them.

"It's Tenas Mowitch!" Tommy exclaimed; then he quickly put his hand over his mouth, realizing he might frighten the fawn.

"How can you tell?" Chet scoffed. "All fawns look alike at that age."

"It is Tenas Mowitch," Tommy insisted. "Don't scare him. Maybe he'll come to me."

Joe and Chet sat on the fallen tree as Tommy walked toward the fawn slowly, holding out his hand and talking softly.

"Don't you remember me, Tenas Mowitch? It's Tommy. I won't hurt you, little fellow."

The fawn trembled and backed away. But it didn't run. Tommy stopped and whispered encouragement to it, then moved forward very slowly. The fawn stretched out its neck to sniff at the extended hand, then came closer to press its nose against it. Tenas Mowitch certainly remembered him and didn't dodge when Tommy reached his other hand out to scratch the fawn behind the ear. Tommy moved his hand along the fawn's slender neck to pet its shoulder. The fawn nestled against him trustingly when his arm slipped around it. It watched as Chet and Joe quietly approached, but it didn't struggle. The fawn seemed to recognize Chet and to sense gentleness and friendliness in Joe.

"I guess I don't want to climb The Mountain," Tommy said. "I'm going to take him to camp."

"Dad won't like it," Chet said dubiously, "but I don't know what else we can do. We can't leave it up here all alone. A wolf or coyote would certainly get it, and if that doesn't happen, it will starve to death."

"You and Joe go ahead," Tommy suggested. "I can find my way back to camp."

"It's better if we go with you," Joe replied. "We can climb The Mountain tomorrow."

Tommy carried the fawn in his arms and walked along the outer edge of the bench, keeping as far away from the bones as he possibly could. That doe was a good mother, and if Dad had let him keep the fawn in camp, she would have stayed close to it, and the wolf wouldn't have killed her. Tommy felt a little resentment, but also realized that his dad couldn't have known this would happen to her. Tommy's arms were getting tired, so he set the fawn on its feet. It trotted along very close to him.

Back at the camp, Dad agreed that Tommy couldn't have left the fawn up on The Mountain alone. He seemed to feel he was stuck with it and might as well make the best of it. Some of the loggers grumbled and predicted trouble, but even so, they made a pet of Tenas Mowitch. Peg Leg fed the fawn cabbage, lettuce, and potato peels. He called it dessert when he added oatmeal with canned milk to the deer's meal. Black Jim, the blacksmith, made a bed for him in the corner of the shop where he could sleep safely at night.

Everything went well for a few days. Tenas Mowitch was friendly but also mischievous. Someone went off and left a bunkhouse door open. There were rows of bunks along the walls, and most of the loggers had nailed boxes over them to hold their shaving kits, writing materials, tobacco, and knickknacks. Tenas Mowitch jumped up on a bunk and then walked the entire length of the bunkhouse, up one side and down the other, eating every bit of tobacco that wasn't sealed in tin cans. Tommy was afraid it would make the deer sick, but there was no problem. Most of the loggers threatened to commit mayhem on Tenas Mowitch if it ever happened again, but Dad gave them all free tobacco and they were satisfied for a while.

Another time, the fawn followed Tommy and Chet out on the boom pond where Pinky was walking along a boomstick with an eighty-pound chain on his shoulder. Tenas Mowitch walked out to meet him, and Pinky couldn't get past. When he tried to push the fawn off the stick, they both fell in the water. The heavy chain turned Pinky upside down in the water and scraped the side of his head before he could get rid of it. He came up sputtering and cursing, but when he got back to the winch raft, he caught Tenas Mowitch's ear and helped the mischief-maker out of the water.

The fawn's worst prank came on the evening before the gas boat was due, the one that would take Tommy and Chet to Ocean Falls, which was the first leg of the journey back to Vancouver. Tenas Mowitch got into the dining room while Tommy and the loggers were all washing up for supper. Tommy didn't miss his little friend until the deer ran past him with Peg Leg close behind him, sputtering and waving a cleaver.

"If you don't keep that pesky varmint out of my cookhouse, I'll make venison stew out of it," Peg Leg roared.

It was some time before Tommy could find out what had happened. Spike told him that the deer had sneaked in, leaped up on a bench, and stood with his forefeet on the table. He ate an entire bowl of lettuce before Peg Leg saw him.

Tommy sat on the beach with Chet, Joe, and Pinky after supper. "What will happen to him when we're gone?" Tommy moaned.

"I'd take him home," Joe said, "only if I did, some of my people would probably eat him this winter."

"He won't be so danged popular around here," Pinky grinned, "but he'll soon learn to keep out of places where he don't belong. I reckon he'll be here when you come back next summer, if Peg Leg doesn't chop his tail off right up close behind his ears."

The comment was Pinky's attempt at humor, but Tommy didn't think it was funny at all.

The gas boat came in after dark and tied up to the boom. The two men who made up the crew were in the office visiting with Dad. Chet was visiting with Pinky in the bunkhouse. Joe had gone home. It was the right moment for Tommy to act on a plan he had developed.

With a flashlight in his pocket and a light coil of line over his shoulder, Tommy slipped quietly out of the room at the corner of the cookhouse storeroom and opened the blacksmith shop door. He murmured something under his breath to Tenas Mowitch, who followed him out across the boom. They moved to where the gas boat was tied up and Tommy lifted the fawn—heavier than Tommy remembered—onto the deck. The cargo hatch was battened down, so he removed the chocks, the canvas cover, and then opened the hatch.

He didn't use his flashlight until he was down in the hold. There was nothing stored there but a pile of boom chains and coils of rope. Tommy lifted the fawn down and used the rope he had brought to tie him to a boom chain. He noticed the door into the engine room was open, so he closed it and hoped no one would remember that it had been left open. Then Tommy kneeled for a long time, holding Tenas Mowitch in his arms. "You keep quiet," he warned. "If they find you before we get to Ocean Falls, they'll probably throw you overboard."

Tommy hadn't made any plans beyond Ocean Falls, and he had no idea what would happen as he replaced the hatch and slipped back to his room. Dad would be angry, he was sure of that, but maybe he would let them take the fawn down to the school. The kids would love Tenas Mowitch, and the school grounds would be a safe place for a young deer. Anyway, he couldn't leave the fawn here for Peg Leg to make into venison stew.

Because Dad had business in Ocean Falls, he accompanied his sons on the first part of their journey home. Tommy was scared and found it hard to keep from crying when he said goodbye to the loggers. Things always looked different in the daytime. Last night in the dark everything seemed fairly simple. Now he kept thinking of all the things that could go wrong. Black Jim might open the blacksmith shop door before they got away, and he'd notice the fawn was missing. Tommy headed across the boom with the boat's crew. The hatch looked all right, and no one could know that it had been opened. After he boarded the boat, he saw Joe coming alongside in his canoe to say goodbye.

"I'll see you next summer," Joe called as the motor started rumbling and the lines were taken in. "Maybe I will trap the old wolf this winter. I'll give you his hide."

Tommy stood on the afterdeck and watched the camp and Joe's canoe dropping farther and farther away. He lost sight of them as the boat swung out of the lagoon through the narrow channel and headed down South Bentinck. Vacation was over for nine long months. There was nothing ahead but school. *And maybe Tenas Mowitch*, he thought, breathing a little easier. If the fawn made a little noise now, maybe no one would hear it over the sound of the engine.

They were pulling into Dean Inlet about noon when Smithy, the engineer, came on deck leading Tenas Mowitch. Tommy's father looked at him. "All right, my boy, let's hear you explain this," he said sternly, but the corners of his lips were twitching, and he didn't look really mad.

"Peg Leg would have killed him," Tommy explained.

Then his father laughed. "I suppose I would have done the same thing when I was ten. The game warden won't let you keep him at Hastings Academy, but I'll ask him to send the fawn down to Stanley Park in Vancouver. They will be glad to take him. There's a big enclosure in the park where he can roam with other deer and no predator can hurt him. You can go out to visit on weekends."

Tommy's arms were around the fawn and tears dropped onto the spotted coat. His father's arm was around both of them.

"I really do know how you feel, Tommy," he said gently. "I had a bear cub when I was a kid. The folks wouldn't let me keep it, so he is in Stanley Park now. A big bear named Tar Baby. Toss him an apple for me next time you visit the park."